It was like a ... *dare believe* ...

As his wife, Oliv... ...ould return to uptown New Orleans and hold her head high. She could hostess luncheons, chair fund-raising committees, come into her own again. She could be happy and fulfilled.

It was a heady thought that he, Reeves Talbot, once merely the servants' son in her family's mansion, could give Olivia all that.

And the unbelievable irony of the whole situation was that, in return, he would have her....

Dear Reader,

Welcome to Silhouette **Special Edition** . . . welcome to romance. Each month Silhouette **Special Edition** publishes six novels with you in mind—stories of love and life, tales that you can identify with . . . as well as dream about.

This month has some wonderful stories for you— after all, March comes in like a lion and goes out like a lamb! And in Lisa Jackson's new series, MAVERICKS, we meet three men who just won't be tamed! This month, don't miss *He's Just a Cowboy* by Lisa Jackson.

THAT SPECIAL WOMAN!, Silhouette **Special Edition**'s new series that salutes women, has a wonderful book this month from Patricia Coughlin. *The Awakening* is the tender story of Sara Marie McAllister—and her awakening to love when she meets bounty hunter John Flynn. It takes a very special man to win That Special Woman! And handsome Flynn is up for the challenge!

Rounding out this month are books from other favorite writers: Elizabeth Bevarly, Susan Mallery, Trisha Alexander and Carole Halston!

I hope that you enjoy this book, and all the stories to come! Have a wonderful March!

Sincerely,

Tara Gavin
Senior Editor
Silhouette Books

CAROLE HALSTON

THE PRIDE OF ST. CHARLES AVENUE

Silhouette®

SPECIAL EDITION®

Published by Silhouette Books New York

America's Publisher of Contemporary Romance

SILHOUETTE BOOKS
300 East 42nd St., New York, N.Y. 10017

THE PRIDE OF ST. CHARLES AVENUE

ISBN: 0-373-09800-6

First Silhouette Books printing March 1993

Printed in the U.S.A.

Books by Carole Halston

Silhouette Special Edition

Keys to Daniel's House #8
Collision Course #41
The Marriage Bonus #86
Summer Course in Love #115
A Hard Bargain #139
Something Lost, Something Gained #163
A Common Heritage #211
The Black Knight #223
Almost Heaven #253
Surprise Offense #291
Matched Pair #328
Honeymoon for One #356
The Baby Trap #388
High Bid #423
Intensive Care #461
Compromising Positions #500
Ben's Touch #543
Unfinished Business #567
Courage To Love #642
Yours, Mine and . . . Ours #682
The Pride of St. Charles Avenue #800

Silhouette Romance

Stand-In Bride #62
Love Legacy #83
Undercover Girl #152
Sunset in Paradise #208

Silhouette Books

To Mother with Love 1992
"Neighborly Affair"

CAROLE HALSTON

is a Louisiana native residing in a rural area north of New Orleans. She enjoys traveling with her husband to research less familiar locations for settings but is always happy to return home to her own unique region, a rich source in itself for romantic stories about warm, wonderful people.

Lake Pontchartrain

EASTERN N.O.

METAIRIE

Canal Street

Vets. Mem. Blvd.

Rt. 10

THE FRENCH
QUARTER

Rt. 90

Jackson

St. Charles Avenue

The Mississippi River

WEST BANK

NEW ORLEANS

N

Prologue

Down on his knees at the Prescott mansion on St. Charles Avenue, twelve-year-old Reeves Talbot worked at a steady pace, weeding the extensive flower beds in the rear gardens. It was a job he detested, but he was doing it of his own free will, to earn the wages he would be paid. Reeves was saving up to buy a bicycle by the end of summer.

His father and his mother might be servants to the rich, elderly Prescotts, but he wasn't a servant to them and neither was his younger sister, Doreen. The fact that home was the renovated carriage house behind the mansion didn't put the Talbot children under any obligation other than to be polite and well behaved. The only reason Reeves had been pressed into service as errand boy and gardener's helper and general flunky this summer was because he'd asked to be.

Right this minute he could be at New Orleans City Park with his buddies, playing touch football and going swimming. He could be at the Audubon Zoo, only a few minutes' ride down St. Charles on the streetcar. He had the price of admission and spending money to buy popcorn and a cold drink. Sheer determination kept him at his labor. He wanted the bicycle he'd picked out at Sears, but there was more involved than just getting something he wanted.

Reeves had set a goal for himself. He would accomplish that goal. It was a matter of character and pride.

If he accumulated the amount of money needed and decided to put it to a better use, that would be different. In any case, he might as well put thoughts of City Park and the Audubon Zoo out of his head and not torture himself. He was stuck here most of the day, grubbing in the dirt.

Reeves wiped his sweaty forehead with a grimy hand and crawled farther along.

"Catch, Reeves!" The childish command came from behind him.

He glanced irritably over his shoulder at seven-year-old Olivia Prescott, who had evidently returned from the birthday party she'd attended that morning, driven in the Prescotts' limousine by Reeves's father, Charles Talbot. She held a large colorful ball in both hands. The bright sunlight glinted off her black ringlets. Dressed in a frilly pink frock, she made an undeniably pretty sight.

It was no wonder that her doting grandparents pampered her. She looked like a little princess in a storybook. Reeves's English-immigrant parents treated her with the gentle deference they might have shown a small member of the British Royal Family.

Even so, he didn't treat Olivia with deference. She was a rich little kid, born with a silver spoon in her mouth, but that didn't mean he had to cater to her. This was America and there was no ruling class. Reeves didn't bow and scrape to anybody, including Olivia's grandparents. He was respectful toward them, as he was toward all adults, but not any *more* respectful than he was to the postman or the deliverymen who used the rear entrance of the mansion.

"Can't you see that I'm busy, Olivia?" Reeves spoke in the same brusque tone he might have used with his younger sister in a similar situation. "I'm not being paid to baby-sit."

Ignoring his words, she tossed the ball to him. With a lithe, athletic twist of his upper body, he easily caught it in one hand and flipped it back to her along the ground. "Didn't you hear me?" he demanded. "Go play somewhere else and don't bother me."

Resuming his hated task, he yanked at a tender weed sprout. It broke off, leaving the roots in the ground, so that he had to dig into the soil with his fingers. Behind him Olivia giggled, and the sound deepened his irritation. Then the ball landed in the flower bed near him with a light *plop*.

She wasn't taking no for an answer. If he wouldn't voluntarily play with her, she would stay here and pester him. And there wasn't a thing that Reeves could do about it. He didn't dare use brute force with her. To go to the mansion and lodge a complaint went completely against his grain.

The frustration was suddenly overwhelming out of all proportion. Reeves had to *do* something physical to vent his fury or else burst. Picking up the ball, he rose to his feet and hurled it with all his strength in the direction of the mansion.

"I'm *not* going to play with you, Olivia. Not now. Not any other time," he informed her harshly.

Her lip quivered, and her eyes filled with tears. "Why are you always mean to me, Reeves?" she asked in a puzzled, hurt voice.

"I'm not mean to you," Reeves denied stoutly, already regretting his display of temper.

"Yes, you are. You're nicer to Doreen than you ever are to me. Sometimes you play with her."

"Doreen's my sister. And I don't play with her a lot. I'm a boy, and boys don't like to play girls' games. Look, I'm sorry if I acted mean," he apologized gruffly. "But you were making a pest out of yourself and interrupting me. I'm earning money this summer to buy a bicycle."

"I could ask my grandpa to buy you a bicycle," she offered. Her expression was wistful as she glanced away into the distance at her ball, and then at Reeves. "Then you wouldn't have to work. You could play with me a little while."

"I'd rather pay for my own. I don't need charity. He wouldn't buy me one, anyway," he added in a hard voice, keeping back the rest of his thought: Old man Prescott might be rolling in money, but he was a tightwad.

"I'm going to go right now and ask him. Then I'll come back and tell you." She was running to carry out her mission as she stated her intention, calling back over her small shoulder.

"Olivia, I told you I don't *want*—" Reeves broke off midsentence as she tripped and pitched forward. His hands lifted in a helpless motion as though by some miracle he might catch her before she hit the hard ground. Paralyzed by his alarm, he stood rooted to the spot, gazing at her still, limp little form. Finally she began crying in pain.

"Olivia." He spoke her name with gruff concern as he went quickly to her, knelt and attempted ever so gently to pick her up and stand her on her feet. But she was a tiny, crumpled deadweight. Awkwardly he gathered her into his arms and held her against his chest, murmuring comforting words. The tenderness in his own voice was embarrassing.

"Now there. You'll be all right. Don't cry, Olivia."

Her crying gradually quieted, but she seemed perfectly content for Reeves to continue to hold her. His discomfort grew more acute as the convulsive sniffles jarring her delicate frame became less frequent. It put him at a terrible disadvantage somehow to feel protective toward her like this.

"Maybe next time you'll be more careful," he said, setting her on her feet with a gentleness that belied the brusqueness of his tone. Rising, he backed away several steps. "Now go inside and play with your toys."

She was a woebegone sight with her tear-streaked face and the pink ribbon in her hair askew. His dirty hands had left brown smudges on her frilly dress. Reeves had to steel himself against an instinctive sympathy allied with some regret he didn't understand. Olivia certainly didn't need sympathy or kindness from him. You didn't feel sorry for a princess.

"I have to get back to work," he said, turning to go back to the flower bed he'd abandoned.

Down on his knees once again, he glanced around and saw her trudging toward the mansion, her silky black curls bouncing against her small back. Briefly he struggled with the impulse to compromise his principles and cater to her. It wouldn't hurt to take a short break and entertain her for a few minutes.

No. Reeves had a goal set for himself, and he needed to stick to his own schedule. If he played with Olivia once, he would be setting a bad precedent.

He didn't want to be wrapped around her little finger.

Nine years later...

Reeves would sure like to have had the amount of money it was costing to throw Olivia's Sweet Sixteen birthday party. Old man Prescott was shelling out enough in one evening to see him through his last year of college. After college he intended to enter law school immediately. So it would still be years before he had the luxury of a free weekend.

Tonight he would have liked to be partying himself. Instead, he was here at Olivia's birthday party, one of the hired help, dressed in garb that made him look like a damned waiter in an opera—black slacks, white blousy shirt and a bright red sash.

It was an outdoor affair held on the rear lawn of the mansion, a soiree that would be written up in the society section of the *Times-Picayune* with a list of the rich teenagers in attendance. Earlier, a newspaper photographer, a young guy in his twenties, had been there snapping pictures. He'd commented with grudging admiration to Reeves, "You can only stage a class act like this one with old money. You spend the same amount in new money, not a penny more or a penny less, and you end up looking pretentious."

Reeves had nodded in indifferent agreement. Coming from his background, he was too used to seeing old money spent to be impressed by lavish entertainment. While he wasn't filled with class resentment like Doreen was, he questioned whether a lot of old money *and* new money couldn't be put to better use.

Well, it was old man Prescott's money, and he hadn't spared any expense throwing a party for his grand-daughter on her sixteenth birthday. Several large canopies were set up. The top rock-and-roll band in New Orleans had been hired to play. The food served would please the palate of a gourmet. Reeves, who regularly tended bar for Olivia's grandparents at their more sedate society gatherings, officiated over an heirloom crystal punch bowl, keeping it replenished with nonalcoholic punch.

He knew darned well that the crystal cups of punch were being liberally spiked on the sly, as were the fancy concoctions he mixed on request, the most popular being frozen strawberry daiquiris minus the rum. Or *supposedly* minus the rum. He kept his expression bland. It wasn't his job to be a chaperon.

Girlish giggles grew shriller and boyish guffaws louder. Flirtatious smiles at Reeves became more and more brazen. Somewhat to his amusement, he found himself thronged by tipsy, teenaged sirens engaging in safe group seduction. Polite and imperturbable, he fielded personal questions and declined invitations to dance.

Olivia wasn't a member of his fan club, and apparently his popularity with her girlfriends didn't please her. He caught her glancing over with a hint of reproval, as though he were at fault. Reeves met the glances calmly, without apology. When she didn't come over and take him to task, he was almost disappointed, which rather annoyed him.

It annoyed him a little, too, that he found himself keeping track of her all night. Pretty as a little girl, she was a knockout as a teenager, and he enjoyed looking at her. The dress she wore was the same bright red color as his sash. Her slim shoulders were bare except for satin cords that served as straps. Reeves felt a pang of male envy watching her dance slow dances in the arms of gawky youths.

Hell, no normal twenty-one-year-old man could fail to appreciate that she was nubile at sixteen with a small-breasted, leggy figure. Heaven help the male population in a few more years, he reflected. She would undoubtedly grow up into a gorgeous woman, sexy but also stylish and classy. Reeves couldn't help but admire the grace with which she carried herself now. That well-bred air must be genetic because it had been evident from childhood.

When Olivia turned eighteen, he would still be in his early twenties. The five years' difference in age wouldn't pose the same gap in maturity. But it might as well. He wouldn't ever date Olivia. She would always be out of his sphere. After her graduation from the exclusive girls' academy she attended, she would be presented formally in society. Her escorts to various debutante balls and parties would be young men from her kind of background.

This was America, truly a land of opportunity, but a New Orleans debutante was out of reach to the son of servants. Class distinctions existed. What was the use in denying it? What was the point in resenting it? Reeves had decided a long time ago to focus his energies and emotions on attaining the attainable.

From birth there had been an invisible line separating himself and Doreen from Olivia. They couldn't be her equal playmates as children. They would have had to defer to her. Under those terms, Reeves had refused to be her playmate at all.

He'd chosen to voluntarily stay on his side of the class line. That had been and was his means of maintaining his self-esteem.

Tonight he didn't treat these rich kids with any more respect because of who their parents were. Nor did he treat them with veiled contempt. It would have been violating his personal code not to show them as much tolerance as he would have shown any group of teenagers.

When Olivia headed toward him at midnight, he didn't sense any new threat to his detachment. The birthday girl had been imbibing, too. He noted the slight unsteadiness in her graceful gait, the flushed color of her cheeks.

"Could I speak to you in private, Reeves?"

The request took him by surprise. "You can say whatever it is you want to say in front of your party guests," he replied.

"Please," she said softly. "I don't want an audience."

It dawned on him then that Olivia was coming on to him. His reaction disturbed him. He wasn't amused, as he had been by the flirting advances of her teenybopper friends. He was irked. And *pleased.*

"I'm one of the hired help, Olivia," he pointed out evenly. "If your grandfather came out, he would expect to see me on the job."

"He doesn't stay up this late. And I would take responsibility," she assured him. "Just this once, couldn't you be nice to me? It's my birthday."

Clasping his arm, she tugged lightly. He let her lead him behind a large potted plant.

"What have you been drinking?" Reeves inquired.

"Champagne," she admitted. "Dom Pérignon."

"You kids are drinking Dom Pérignon?" A note of frank indignation crept into his voice, exposing more than he cared to reveal, but, fortunately, she seemed to construe it as a note of reprisal.

"You won't tell my grandfather?"

He shrugged. "It's none of my business. Now you'd better get back to your party and let me get back to my job."

She ignored his words. He could sense her gathering her courage as she stepped closer to him and placed her palms on his chest.

"Do you have a steady girlfriend?" she asked, her voice soft and seductive.

"No, I don't."

Her perfume was flowery and feminine. One of her satin cord straps slid slowly down her arm. The thought of easing it back up on her shoulder awoke a male anticipation. Reeves stood his ground and spoke her name brusquely.

"Olivia."

"You always used that rough tone of voice with me," she accused, pouting prettily. "Why? Was the reason that you didn't want me to like you?"

"It might have been. How do I know? And what difference does it make?"

"Why don't you have a girlfriend? You're so tall and good-looking." She slid her hands up to his shoulders, moving even closer until their bodies were almost touching. "Do you date lots of different girls?"

"When I date, I date women, not girls. And that's very seldom because I don't have the spare time or the money. Plus I drive an old rattletrap of a car. Now behave yourself and go flirt with some boy your own age."

"If you took me out, we could use my new car that I got for my birthday. You could drive."

She'd gotten a sporty little convertible, a dream of a car. It had been delivered earlier in the evening by the dealer and presented to her by her grandparents.

"I don't *want* to take you out. You're too young. And besides, your grandfather wouldn't allow it."

"He wouldn't have to know. We could meet and have secret dates. I have a big allowance. I could pay part...or all."

Reeves grasped her hands and took them down from his shoulders. "You'll have to find yourself another gigolo," he informed her harshly. "Frankly I'm not interested in rich, spoiled little girls."

She drooped before his eyes, like a vivid crushed blossom. Reeves felt ashamed of himself and irritated because he was a sap for feeling like a brute. Why shouldn't she encounter some hard reality. Tonight she'd been sipping Dom Pérignon. A bottle cost more than his wages for a whole evening's work, an evening when he would have liked to be sipping beer with his peers.

Still he had been harder on her than was justified. If any one of the other teenaged girls at the party had pulled him off behind a potted plant, he would have dealt with the situation differently. That realization bothered Reeves.

"Look," he said, "I'm flattered. I really am. You're very pretty, as I'm sure you know. A lot of guys would jump at the chance."

"You think I'm pretty?"

"If I didn't, I wouldn't have said it." Her other strap had slid down, thanks to the dejected slope of her smooth, bare shoulders.

"Do you know what I wished for tonight when I blew out the candles on my birthday cake?"

Reeves let his silence serve as an answer: What on earth was there for her to wish for?

Olivia went on quickly, breathlessly, as though needing to hurry before her courage failed her. "I wished that before the night was over, you would take me into your arms and kiss me."

She tilted her head back, her long curly lashes lowered. Then she raised them to gaze up at him in lovely invitation.

"Won't you make my wish come true, Reeves?" she asked softly.

It was an innocent request on the surface, inconsequential, but fraught with deeper, grim significance for him. On a whim, Olivia wanted him to step over the invisible line that separated them, the line of demarcation that allowed him to work at the Prescott mansion, but never be an invited guest. She was granting him permission to break the rule *Look, but don't touch.*

Just as easily, she could slap the restriction on him again, put him in his place. It was the identical situation that had existed when she was a little girl and wanted him to play with her. Then he wouldn't have had any rights. Nor did he have any now.

Reeves was insulted and angered by the underlying implications. It made him all the more resentful that he couldn't allow himself the pleasure of taking her into his arms and kissing her.

"You wouldn't like the way I kissed you," he warned her in a callous voice. "A man doesn't kiss like a sixteen-year-old boy."

"Kiss me the same way you kiss your dates," she implored with a little shiver.

"Remember, you asked for this," Reeves said.

Without any gentleness he framed her face between his palms, brought his mouth to hers and kissed her with hard, grinding pressure. She gasped in helpless reaction, giving him entry. Taking advantage, he sought out her tongue with his and inflicted more intimate abuse.

A whimpering sound in her throat brought a halt. Reeves pulled back, his flare of anger fast dissipating.

"There. Are you satisfied?" he demanded gruffly, overpowering his first instinct, which was to apologize for being a heel.

Her eyes, a beautiful shade of blue tinged with violet, shimmered with unshed tears. She gulped and blinked long, wet lashes, spilling two huge droplets down her cheeks. Reeves had never wanted anything in his life more than he wanted to wipe away those tears with a gentle touch, but he tightened his lowered hands into fists.

"It's no fair turning on the waterworks, Olivia. You can't say that I didn't warn you."

Her soft, bruised mouth quivered. "I should have known better than to hope that you would ever like me. You're mean and horrible. I *hate* you."

Reeves winced at the break in her voice. "Look, I'm sorry," he said gruffly. "But you have to see my side of things."

"I don't have to see *anything!*" she denied, lifting her head to a proud angle. "I wish I didn't ever have to see *you* again after tonight! That's my new birthday wish."

She turned and stalked away with a regal air. Watching her go, Reeves felt admiration. He lifted a hand as though to make an apologetic overture, then dropped it. He'd said that he was sorry, and he was. There was really nothing more to say, no way to undo what was done.

No, but it was in his power to grant her wish not to have to encounter him anymore. Tonight would be his last stint as hired flunky at the Prescott mansion on St. Charles Avenue.

He didn't need this guilt, this resentment.

This regret.

Olivia wasn't scarred for life because he'd rejected her. As rotten as he felt, Reeves knew he'd done the right thing to stay on his side of that invisible class line.

Five more years later...

Striding across the lakefront campus on the way to his ancient Chevrolet, Reeves's only problem in the world at that moment was keeping a silly grin off his face. Happiness was knowing that college and law school were behind him and that he carried a piece of paper in his hip pocket that said he'd passed the Louisiana bar exam on his first try.

A brunette coed cut across his path some thirty yards or so ahead of him. Reeves stopped in his tracks, jolted by surprised recognition.

Was that Olivia Prescott?

It certainly looked like her—or an understated, mature twin. The hairdo was plain, her black hair held at the nape of her neck by a barrette. Her outfit was simple—drab olive slacks and a white blouse. There was that indefinable touch of class, though, in her carriage.

Should he say hello to her? Reeves hesitated a moment, torn. *Why the hell not?* he thought and, changing direction, loped after her in pursuit. When he got near, he slowed down and hailed her. She froze at the sound of her name and slowly turned around, waiting calmly, with no pretense of welcome, while he walked up to her.

"Hello, Reeves."

"It's been a long time, Olivia."

"Yes, it has," she agreed.

"You're enrolled here as a student?" The question was foolishly rhetorical. Obviously she was. She had an armload of textbooks. "I just assumed that you would go ahead and finish up at Newcomb."

Sophie Newcomb College of Women was located in the university district along with Tulane University and Loyola University. All three were old institutions of higher learning steeped in tradition, charging much higher tuition and offering far greater snob appeal than LSUNO, the New Orleans branch of Louisiana State University, located in Metairie.

Reeves continued awkwardly, "I mean, I thought surely..."

"You thought there was a trust fund my grandfather's creditors might not be able to touch. No, there wasn't." She corrected him in a flat tone.

"But your mother and your grandmother were Newcomb alumnae, weren't they? Surely there's an endowment to cover such cases as yours."

"There might be. I didn't check into it. I preferred to transfer here. I'm majoring in business, going to school on a student loan. How are you?" With the polite inquiry, she closed the subject of her altered circumstances and the misfortunes that had befallen her a year ago.

First, her grandmother had died of a stroke. A few short weeks later, old man Prescott had put a gun to his head. Olivia's inheritance had turned out to be a pile of debts. Her grandparents' possessions and the family mansion had been sold at auction. Reeves hadn't realized that she was left penniless.

"I couldn't be better," he admitted. "I finished up my law degree at Loyola last spring and just passed the bar. I came by today to visit one of my professors here who gave me a lot of encouragement."

"Congratulations. I know Esther and Charles must be very proud." A fond note entered her voice at the mention of his parents. "Are they happy living in Florida?"

"Oh, yes. Happy as clams. They're managing a mom-and-pop motel and have an apartment right on the premises. It's an arrangement that suits them to a tee."

"I'm so glad. Please tell them hello for me."

"I'll do that."

"And how is Doreen? Recently I saw an article in the newspaper with her byline."

"Doreen's great," he replied uneasily. His bright, abrasive sister had attended a liberal women's college on scholarship, majoring in journalism. She'd returned to New Orleans even more radical in her politics and views about society. A month ago she'd confided to Reeves that she was digging into old man Prescott's business dealings and private life, and uncovering corruption and scandal that she intended to make public in a shocking exposé once she'd amassed the full information.

He couldn't forewarn Olivia of the unpleasantness in store for her without betraying his sister's confidence.

"Are you doing okay?" he asked gently.

"Yes, I'm doing okay," she answered. "I'm finding out that life does go on after the silver spoon has been taken away. Or sold at auction, as the case may be." She pushed aside a wavy tendril of glossy black hair that had escaped the barrette. Her forced smile didn't lighten the soberness in her extraordinarily beautiful eyes. "Well, I'd better be going. I wish you every success, Reeves. You've certainly earned it. It couldn't have been easy, moving out on your own at eighteen and putting yourself through college and law school. Goodbye now."

"Are you headed to class?" he asked, reluctant to say goodbye.

"No, I'm on my way to the library."

"Could I buy you a cup of coffee?"

"No, thank you," she said simply.

Reeves tried not to show how rebuffed he felt. He backed away a step. "Well, take care."

"You do the same. Goodbye."

She turned and continued on her way, leaving him standing there and gazing after her, coping with his disappointment.

Damn, he wished he hadn't seen her today.

In a deflated mood, Reeves headed once again for the parking lot.

Chapter One

"Here's the society section."

Judy Hays, Olivia's apartment mate, pulled out the crisp, folded section from the bulky Sunday edition of the *Times-Picayune*. The two women were in their robes, having just sat down to read the newspaper with freshly poured mugs of coffee near at hand. Olivia was on the sofa and Judy sat in a wingback chair that was comfortable as well as elegant.

"I'm not dying to read the society news," Olivia protested with good-natured exasperation. "It's not of any more interest to me than it is to you."

"Of course it is. You know most of the people mentioned. They're total strangers to me." Undeterred, Judy sailed the section over to the sofa.

"I wish you didn't insist on believing that deep down I'm longing to be back on St. Charles Avenue and in the middle of the social whirl. I'm *not*."

"You're not *longing* to live on St. Charles Avenue again. I don't think that. I admire you, Olivia, because of the way you've adjusted and made the best of things. But you can live your life here in Metairie, and you'll always be a fish out of water. You belong in uptown New Orleans."

"I'm no more a fish living out of water than you are. You grew up in Ponchatoula." Ponchatoula was a small rural town about an hour's drive from New Orleans.

"Not *in* Ponchatoula." Judy corrected her ruefully. "Our farm is five miles out of town."

"You agree with the point I'm making, though."

"One word out of my mouth, and it's obvious that I'm from the country," the other woman conceded with a cheerful grin. She sipped her coffee. "But I moved to the big city to escape small-town life. I love all this tacky, urban congestion. Can you honestly say that you do?"

"No, I don't love it," Olivia had to admit. "But I'm happy with my lot in life. I have a good-paying job and friends and a satisfying social life."

They'd had essentially this same conversation more than once during the past couple of years, the length of time that they'd shared an apartment. Olivia always felt as though she were being put on the defensive. It seemed necessary for some reason to convince Judy that she didn't have the mentality of a deposed princess living in exile.

"You should have friends with all the favors that you do for people. I'll bet you have a wedding or a shower or some other event to attend this afternoon and supervise."

"A bridal shower." Olivia picked up the society section and glanced at the front page.

"I'm telling you, you're missing a bet not starting a business as a social consultant. You could charge for all that free advice..." Judy's voice drifted off as she became engrossed in an article.

Olivia didn't reply. They'd had this conversation before, too. Maybe it was a lack of enterprise on her part, but the idea of charging people for giving them the benefit of her background seemed mercenary. Her salary earned working in the claims department of a large insurance company was sufficient. She didn't feel the need to earn extra income.

Judy meant well, Olivia realized. Having grown up in a large family where money had always been scarce, she put more value on wealth, interestingly enough, than Olivia did. Olivia regarded money as merely a necessary commodity. She knew from painful experience that it was a tool of capricious fortune. All the things that it could buy, not just material possessions, but intangibles like social position, could so easily be snatched away.

Never again would Olivia let her happiness be contingent on wealth. There was too much risk.

Judy's fish analogy was wrong, she reflected, turning the page. Olivia wasn't a fish out of water in Metairie. She was a fish from a fancy aquarium released into a large, anonymous, teeming pond.

Familiar faces smiled back at her from photographs taken at a black-tie affair. Before looking at the pictures individually, Olivia scanned the first paragraph of the society column to determine the occasion, a big fundraiser for Children's Hospital. It was an annual society event, Olivia knew, a pet project of Marcia Hymer's. She and Marcia had been friends from childhood and inseparable during the years that they'd both attended *the* exclusive girls' school in uptown New Orleans.

Searching for Marcia, she found her standing arm in arm with her husband, Clinton, who, in his tuxedo, looked like a well-dressed teddy bear. Next to them were William and Debra Sue Duplantis. Olivia's gaze rested on William an extra second until a disturbing twinge of recognition had subsided. He was also an important person out of her past, the man she had been engaged to marry, when her world fell apart. It was only human to feel some emotion at the sight of him. At least the emotion wasn't bitter—a healthy sign.

Olivia moved on to the fifth person in the snapshot, a tall, urbane, dark-haired man in his early thirties, smiling directly into the camera. She blinked and gazed hard, hit by another jolt of recognition just as unpleasant and, oddly enough, stronger.

"What is it?" Judy inquired curiously, apparently having looked up and noticed her friend's expression.

Olivia answered in the tone of one who was stating an amazing fact. "Reeves Talbot was a guest at Marcia Hymer's annual fund-raiser for Children's Hospital."

"So. Who is he?"

"He's the son of the English couple who were employed by my grandparents."

"You mean Esther and Charles, the housekeeper and the chauffeur." Judy easily provided the names. She was endlessly fascinated by the story of Olivia's background, finding it highly glamorous in comparison to her own. "That's right. They had two children, a boy and a girl. You've never had much to say about him. She got a scholarship to a top women's college, came back and went to work as a reporter, then dug up all that dirt on your grandfather after he died, and ruined his good name."

"Doreen." Olivia spoke the name with absentminded loathing, all her attention still fixed on the newspaper.

"I'm trying to remember. Did he become a lawyer?"

"Yes."

"My curiosity is killing me." Judy came over and perched on the edge of the sofa next to Olivia. "Show me his picture."

Olivia pointed Reeves out.

Her apartment mate whistled appreciatively. "He's good-looking enough to be my hunk-of-the-month any old month of the year. I'm surprised you blocked him out of your memory."

"I had a crush on him from the time I was a little girl." The recollection was factual, not reminiscent. When Olivia talked about her past, she always used that same tone of voice, as though she were speaking of someone else, someone who no longer existed. "He could never be bothered to show me any attention."

"He was older than you, wasn't he?"

"Five years older. He must be thirty-four now."

Judy shrugged. "Five years between kids is a lot and especially between a boy and a girl, when he's the older one. You might have just been a pain in the butt to him," she suggested matter-of-factly. "Who are these other people in the picture?" Judy read the caption aloud. "'Chairwoman Marcia Hymer With Banker Hubby, Clinton, Prominent Attorney William Duplantis III, And Wife Debra Sue'—isn't he your old fiancé?"

"Not strictly speaking. William and I weren't formally engaged."

"But he'd asked you to marry him, and you'd said yes."

Olivia nodded, her mind more on the present. How on earth had Reeves Talbot gotten his name on an invitation list that would read like the Who's Who of New Orleans society? What law firm had he joined anyway? she wondered. Surely not one of the prestigious old downtown firms like Duplantis & Duplantis, not with a public school education and no social connections. A junior partnership in Duplantis & Duplantis had been William's birthright.

"I'll call Marcia and solve this whole mystery," she said, thinking aloud.

"Find out Reeves Talbot's phone number, why don't you? Then you can call him up and talk over old times and casually mention yours truly, this gorgeous blond friend who's watched every episode of 'Upstairs Downstairs' on PBS."

Olivia didn't smile at the facetious suggestion. She was scanning the society column.

"Is there any mention of a wife or a fiancée?" Judy inquired, returning to her chair.

"No. It says here, 'Handsome Bachelor Reeves Talbot.' Apparently he wasn't escorting anyone." That would have been the obvious explanation of how he'd been included. "I would never have taken Reeves for a social climber," Olivia reflected.

"I'm surprised that New Orleans high society has gotten that democratic."

"So am I."

"Unless he's come up with a fake background for himself. But wouldn't your old friends from uptown recognize him?"

"It's possible that they wouldn't." Olivia frowned thoughtfully. "Actually, the last time they might have seen him was at my Sweet Sixteen birthday party. He was one of the hired staff. After that, he was never around. I'm twenty-nine so it's been, what, thirteen years."

"Did something happen at the party? I seem to detect a pained note in your voice."

Olivia grimaced. "Yes. There was an unpleasant incident with him and me. I'll tell you about it sometime."

A few minutes later, giving up on concentrating on any other news printed in the newspaper, she took the society section with her into her bedroom, where she could call Marcia on her phone extension and have a private conversation. She had Marcia and Clint's unlisted home number, along with other unlisted numbers of members of her old group.

There had been a period when she cut off all contact, but Marcia and also Sissy Bella had persisted in trying to keep in touch. Now, a few times each year, she got together with them and one or two more of her former classmates and fellow debutantes, usually for birthday luncheons. On rare occasions she got talked into a dinner party.

They would all have gladly welcomed her back into their inner circle, she didn't doubt. From time to time they would try to match her up with an eligible man on the theory that she could easily marry back into New Orleans society. Olivia knew that it wasn't that simple. Too much had happened to her. She was a different person now, with a different perspective and changed values.

Marcia answered on the second ring. "Olivia! This must be telepathy! I just made a mental note to call you

during the week and twist your arm to come to dinner."
Without pause, she demanded, "Have you seen today's
paper?"

"I'm looking at your picture as we speak." The
newspaper rested on Olivia's lap.

"So am I. Please tell me that you didn't recognize me
immediately. I look like a candidate for a face-lift."

"Don't be silly," Olivia said, scoffing. "You look
marvelous."

Abandoning the discussion of the picture, Marcia re-
ported on the huge success of her fund-raiser, the cul-
mination of many months of committee meetings. Then
she came back to the newspaper write-up, an arch note
entering her voice. "In case you're wondering, the man
standing next to William—Reeves Talbot—isn't just
photogenic, my dear. He's that handsome and every bit
as charming."

Olivia wet her lips. They didn't form words to say that
Reeves Talbot was no stranger to her or to Marcia. For
some reason, it was difficult to speak of him.

"Don't tell me that he didn't catch your eye," Marcia chided. "Or I will consider you a lost cause. He came
with William and Debra Sue as their guest. He's an attorney. The rumor is that William is courting him to join
the Duplantis law firm. That's all I know about him.
Well, one other thing."

Marcia's gently apologetic inflection put Olivia at a
loss. It warned her that she might find the bit of additional information about Reeves painful. And yet Marcia obviously didn't know his real identity, that he was
Charles and Esther's son and the despicable, disloyal
Doreen's brother.

"What is it?" Olivia asked.

A reluctant pause heightened the suspense.

"His address."

Further explanation wasn't necessary. Olivia could guess for herself where Reeves lived. Her first reaction was stunned denial, then appalled denial. *No, he wouldn't have the gall.*

"Is his address St. Charles Avenue?" she confirmed, her voice taut with outrage.

Marcia's sigh of sympathy came over the line. "Yes. Unfortunately. But it's hardly fair to hold it against him, Olivia, that it's your old address. For you and for me, turning your grandparents' home into condominiums was a terrible desecration, but the developers were the guilty parties. On the bright side, the buildings and grounds are beautifully maintained rather than being allowed to deteriorate. The days are long gone when even the wealthy can afford the upkeep on a huge mansion."

With no knowledge of who he actually was, Marcia couldn't be expected to understand the underlying implications. Reeves Talbot was expressing the most flagrant contempt for her and her dead grandparents by taking up residence in a mutilated portion of the Prescott mansion. He was thumbing his nose at her upbringing and his. There was no other reasonable explanation. If his real consideration had been comfort and life-style, he could have picked any one of a number of other equally upscale places to live in New Orleans.

Underneath that handsome appearance, he was as petty and spiteful as his sister, Doreen, the one person in the whole world Olivia had ever detested. Before now.

Now she detested him, too.

"I don't suppose that you'd be interested in meeting him," Marcia said with a sad acceptance. "I had feared as much."

The receiver in Olivia's hand shook and the newspaper on her lap rustled with tremors of helpless anger and resentment. She didn't trust herself to reply for fear of unleashing a torrent of hateful words.

Also keeping her mute was another strong emotion that might flare out of control. *Disappointment.* She was disappointed in Reeves.

Marcia was continuing with a faint hopeful note. "I had in mind a small, intimate dinner party. No more than eight or ten at the table. Just a relaxed evening with old friends. Of course, if I plan it for next weekend, Sissy couldn't come. She and George will be out of town, attending a medical convention. Speaking of Sissy, let me tell you her latest fiasco...."

Olivia's emotional turmoil calmed under the lively flow of Marcia's chatter. After all, she'd suffered much more shocking revelations, much more devastating disappointment. This certainly wasn't the first time in her life that she'd been wrong about the male of the species. It really shouldn't come as any great surprise that Reeves Talbot had grown up to be less than admirable.

The heaviest strike against him was that he was evidently ashamed of his humble background and was keeping it secret. His conduct was a disgrace to his parents, who were good, dignified people, if not very well educated.

Olivia could throw a monkey wrench into his social-climbing ambitions. She could expose him for being a sly phony rather than a mystery man, new on the social scene.

But she wouldn't. To be vindictive would be sinking to his level and Doreen's. Let them answer to their own consciences.

I'd like to tell him to his face what I think of him, she thought.

Marcia had wound down. "Back to my dinner party idea, I wouldn't have to invite Reeves. I could invite another single man as your dinner partner."

Olivia took a deep breath, annoyed at her own attack of jitters over what she was about to suggest. "Go ahead and invite this Reeves Talbot. There's just one condition. Don't tell him in advance who the woman is that you're pairing him up with for the evening. Don't play matchmaker."

"Fair enough. That way he can make his own first impressions. He'll be bowled over," Marcia predicted complacently. "I'm expecting love at first sight on his part at the very least."

"I wouldn't count on it," Olivia replied with irony.

The sight of her wouldn't awaken any old fondness in Reeves. That was for sure. Nor did she offer him what he was apparently interested in, an entry into New Orleans society. Her once-impeccable credentials had been revoked.

Meeting him again after so many years wouldn't revive Olivia's old adoration. Of that she was sure. He'd killed it once and for all with his brutal kiss the night of her sixteenth birthday party.

It was odd, though, that looking down at his picture and then at William's, her response to Reeves's likeness was still the more intense reaction.

The Hymer home was on Prytania Street in the historic Garden District of uptown New Orleans. Entering, Olivia appreciated the gracious ambiance. Richly patterned Oriental rugs underfoot, the polished patina of fine furniture, the subdued glitter of chandeliers suspended from high ceilings, fragrant arrangements of fresh flowers—it was all so familiar.

The combined message was *home*.

It awoke a poignant longing that she found disturbing. Was Judy more perceptive than Olivia gave her credit for being? Deep down did Olivia long to return to all of this?

You're just edgy, she told herself. A thousand times she'd regretted impulsively accepting the dinner party invitation.

Catching a glimpse of her reflection in an antique French mirror, Olivia was reassured that she didn't appear the reluctant guest. After much deliberation, she was wearing a simple, elegant black dress and silver jewelry. As a matter of vague principle, she hadn't shopped for anything new to wear or taken any special pains with her appearance. She would dress exactly the same to go out to dinner at a nice restaurant in Metairie.

The farthest thing from her mind had been to make a dramatic entrance, but, as luck would have it, there had been an accident on the interstate, backing up traffic. She was the last to arrive, Marcia had divulged, giving Olivia a warm welcoming embrace. Now she was leading her, arm in arm, to join the rest of the party, chattering on in typical fashion.

"I didn't tell a soul, except Clinton," Marcia confided at the door to her living room. "I kept it a big secret. Isn't that fun? It's going to be a marvelous treat for everyone that I've managed to lure you from the suburbs."

Olivia had her private doubts whether her turning up was going to be a treat for Reeves. He was probably going to suffer a bad moment or two, until his fears about being identified as the son of servants were put to rest. She couldn't feel too sorry for him. He deserved a bad moment or two.

"Look who's here!" Marcia called out, propelling Olivia into the center of her formal, but much-used and inviting living room. The original small, intimate dinner party proposed had grown, a fact for which Olivia was prepared.

The various conversations all stopped. There was a shifting of the vivid mosaic of color in the room as the women, dressed in jewel tones, and men in dark suits or white dinner jackets turned around in response to the announcement. Familiar faces lighted up with surprise and smiles broke out. A chorus of voices, ranging from soprano to baritone, intoned her name with feminine delight or male heartiness. "Olivia!"

Marcia raised one hand in a regal restraining gesture, preventing a general converging upon of Olivia. "As you were, my friends," she commanded gaily. "You'll all get your hug and kiss in due course. First let me do my duty and introduce Olivia to Reeves."

He stood with a small group near the marble fireplace. His companions moved to right and left, opening up a straight avenue so that Olivia had a full view of him from dark hair to dark gleaming shoes. Her heart played traitor, giving a leap of instinctive female approval. In black slacks and white dinner jacket, he managed somehow to be polished and handsome and yet retain the ruggedly masculine quality he'd always had.

Olivia read surprise on his face. His dark brown eyes held a hint of uncertainty. But they also radiated unqualified male admiration. There was none of the wariness that she was expecting, no inkling of dismay. Apparently he was too taken off guard for it to sink in immediately that she might queer his social ambitions tonight, if she were so inclined.

"Hello, Reeves." Olivia greeted him when she and Marcia were several steps away, before Marcia could perform an introduction. Her polite, pleasant tone was the tone she would have used to greet a stranger.

"Hello, Olivia." He moved forward instead of standing his ground, as she would have expected him to do. "It's been a long time. How are you?"

"You two know each other?" Marcia stated the obvious in the form of a rhetorical question, giving Olivia a blankly questioning look that spoke volumes. What was this all about? Why hadn't Olivia mentioned that she was acquainted with him?

He spoke up, saving Olivia from having to answer. "Olivia and I go way back, Marcia."

"It was aeons ago." She addressed her words to Marcia, too, as he had done.

"I'm getting curiouser by the moment," Marcia declared. "Is one of you going to take pity and fill me in, in twenty-five words or less?"

"I'll let Olivia tell you," Reeves said. "I think it's more her story than mine."

"I happen to disagree or I would have told the story already," she replied evenly. He could at least show a little gratitude for her discretion. "Why don't we forget about ancient history and get on with the party?"

Marcia threw up her hands in defeat. "Let the party resume."

Friends crowded around Olivia, eager to say hello. She was conscious that Reeves moved away a little distance, making room for her to hold court. It put a strain on her that he was near, able to observe and listen while she responded to the typical complimentary remarks. Not until he got drawn into his own conversation did she relax a little.

During the hour of socializing before dinner, he didn't compete for his share of her company, not once coming to stand by her side. However, each time that Olivia sneaked a covert glance at him, she seemed to connect with his gaze. It said that he was only biding his time.

This had been a mistake coming here tonight. Olivia realized that, but had no choice but to stick it out through the evening. Seeing Reeves again after all these years had been a foolish impulse. What was the point? Nothing constructive would be gained. Her original urge to confront him and deliver her low opinion of his character had evaporated.

When dinner was announced, he came at once to escort her into the dining room, where he seated her with faultless manners. Olivia smiled at him coolly when he had taken his chair beside her. She was furious with herself because her pulse was racing and her body reacting with pleasure. It came as a personal affront that she found him so attractive.

He and Doreen were two of a kind. He had chosen to move into Olivia's old home. She wrapped herself in the reminder, needing some protective armor against his mere physical proximity.

Their hostess, seated at their end of the long dining room table, focused general attention on them, and issued a gay warning. "Be careful, you two, what you say to each other, because I intend to eavesdrop and solve your mystery relationship."

"It's no big mystery," Reeves began with a touch of reluctance. Hesitantly he glanced at Olivia.

Whether he was seeking direction or asking for her help in evading the issue was unclear. Olivia chose not to gaze into his eyes and carry on any unspoken communication with him.

"You're not a very good detective," she said chidingly to her hostess and old friend. "I'm employed by a large insurance company. I have contact with lots of attorneys."

"I've read enough detective novels to know a red herring," Marcia retorted smilingly. Then she switched her attention elsewhere.

"What insurance company?" Reeves inquired interestedly so that anyone else paying attention to their conversation could rule out the possibility that they'd met in the workplace.

Olivia replied and then answered several more questions that pinpointed the exact nature of her job in the claims department. She could guess what was behind his curiosity. The idea of her working and supporting herself at a job that was anything but glamorous probably tickled him no end.

"What's the name of your law firm?" She eventually got in a question about him and conducted her own interrogation.

He wasn't affiliated with a firm, he explained readily enough. On a case-by-case basis, he teamed up with one or the other of several attorneys in the same office building on Gravier Street, in the downtown business district. They all shared a law library.

Olivia could fill in the blanks for herself. He was a plaintiff lawyer, a euphemistic term for ambulance chaser. The rumor Marcia had heard must not be true. Instead of Duplantis & Duplantis courting Reeves, he was probably angling to get his foot in the door of the highly reputable old firm on any terms that they would offer him.

The profile fit with her disillusioning assessment of his character up until now. Beneath that handsome exterior, he was ambitious, cynical and ruthless, pursuing his own agenda. Obviously his ladder of success involved gaining social prominence, whatever means it took.

Olivia's dinner companion seated on the other side asked her opinion on a topic that apparently was under discussion. She siezed the opportunity to end the private conversation between herself and Reeves, responding to the question and then politely including him.

She didn't care to know any more about him. His address gave the cue to his attitudes and values. It said that he sneered at memories she held dear, that he trampled underfoot daily those same traditions and standards that he'd decided he wanted for himself.

All Olivia asked was to get through the evening and go back to her safe refuge in Metairie. Tonight was a bad experience. A *totally* bad experience. Her rational mind and tense nerves told her plainly, and yet her senses betrayed her.

The sound of Reeves's voice, deep and masculine, awoke pleasure that shivered through her, like the sonorous note of a bass instrument. The sight of his well-shaped hand grasping his fork or lifting his wineglass to his lips met with an innate feminine approval. Repeated stubborn glances over at him didn't lessen the impact of his broad-shouldered, manly presence, didn't strengthen her weak resistance to his clean-cut, but rugged good looks.

Against her will, she reveled in the fact that he was affected similarly by her. *Damn, you're beautiful,* he told her every time they made direct eye contact.

The chemistry between them didn't go undetected by Marcia, who met Olivia's defensive gaze with an arch, smug expression.

At long last, the dessert course was served and Olivia could see the end in sight. Following dinner, she intended to make her departure as soon as it was polite to do so.

Rising from her chair, she added her sincere compliments to the general chorus lauding Marcia for her truly wonderful gourmet meal. Everyone except Reeves, Olivia noticed, commented to the effect that Marcia had outdone herself, as usual. It occurred to her that this must have been his first time as the Hymers' dinner guest.

Had he felt like an outsider? Olivia wondered. She had been so intent on her own feelings that she hadn't given any consideration to his. Certainly he hadn't given any sign of being ill at ease.

The moment's sympathy dissipated with the touch of his fingers, strong and sure, clasping her arm. Amidst the general confusion and milling about, he escorted her from the dining room.

"How about some fresh air?" he suggested.

Before Olivia could reply, he was propelling her toward French doors that opened onto a side porch.

"It might be good to clear the air," she said, mustering her defenses.

Out on the porch, she pulled slightly against his clasp, and he immediately dropped his hand. She led the way to the farthest end. The sweet scent of blooming wisteria perfumed the spring night.

"I was knocked for a loop when you showed up tonight," Reeves remarked when they had come to a standstill at the railing. "But I guess that was pretty apparent."

Olivia replied with a stiff-backed dignity. "It wasn't very fair of me, I admit, to seal Marcia's lips and have her not give you any advance warning. I really wasn't paying you back for all the times that you were mean to me. Or not consciously, anyway."

"I don't recall being *mean* to you," he objected. "I just refused to cater to you, like everyone else did."

"Whatever. It doesn't matter now. You and I won't be running into each other, in case you're worried about that. I live in Metairie and don't travel in this circle. Marcia won't pry any information out of me."

"Marcia is welcome to know any information that you care to tell her. That's one thing I brought you out here to say."

"Then why have you kept quiet about who you are?"

"I haven't kept quiet about who I am," he denied. "If you're under the impression that I've carefully concealed the fact that my parents were servants in the employ of your grandparents, it simply isn't the case."

"You haven't divulged the fact, either. Marcia and Clinton and the others here tonight don't have an inkling."

"Only because they're superficial acquaintances at this point. I don't make a point of giving my family history when I'm introduced to people. That doesn't mean that I'm ashamed of any part of my background. I'm not."

"Don't you feel like an imposter making the acquaintance of someone who isn't a total stranger? Like Marcia, for instance? You must have recognized her. She was one of my closest friends. You must have remembered her."

"No, I didn't remember *her*. I paid very little attention to your friends. I was more interested in my own at
the time."

Olivia wondered about the slight emphasis on *her*.
Who had he remembered? It was irrelevant.

"Well, I'll still leave it up to you to give your own case
history. Now I think we had better mind our manners
and rejoin the party."

He stopped her before she could take a step, reaching
to catch her elbow with a quickness that set off a flash
of déjà vu. For a few seconds she was a little girl again
tossing a ball at him and watching admiringly as he reacted with lightning reflexes to catch it.

"We won't be missed for a few minutes," he urged.
"After all, Marcia invited us both to get us together."

"She didn't realize how ill suited we are for each
other."

"How can you be so certain that we're ill suited? We
don't even know each other as adults."

Olivia's whole arm was tingling from his grasp. She
tugged free and rubbed the area with her palm.

"There's too much bad feeling between us. We could
never be friends, much less more than friends. The one
person in the world that I would wish harm to is your
sister."

"Doreen's exposé of your grandfather," he recalled
in a regretful tone. "I suppose you would have hard
feelings over that. The whole business had slipped my
mind."

"Well, it hasn't slipped mine."

"You can't hold Doreen's actions against me, can
you? I'd like to see you again, Olivia. You're a beautiful, interesting woman."

"But I don't want to see you again, Reeves."

"Why not?" he persisted. "Couldn't you give me the benefit of the doubt and spend one evening in my company?"

"What kind of date did you have in mind?" she asked proudly. "And afterward would you suggest going to your place?"

He sighed. "You know where I live."

"Yes, I do."

"And you're offended by the very idea."

"Yes, I'm offended. Now we really should mind our manners and go inside."

This time he didn't try to stop her. At the French doors, she looked back at him questioningly. He hadn't followed behind her.

"I wonder how many times through the years I've watched you walk off," he mused.

"With any luck, this will be the last time," Olivia replied, thinking to herself that all those exits had had one thing in common: she had walked away from him, feeling rejected.

There was no reason that her exit tonight should have the same quality of defeat. But it did.

Chapter Two

"What's up?" Alan Cramer spoke from the doorway of Reeves's office.

Reeves, seated at his desk with a folder open in front of him, looked up, the abstracted expression on his face turning to welcome at the sight of his friend and associate attorney, whose office was on the same floor.

"Come in." He accompanied the invitation with an expansive arm gesture and sat back in his leather-upholstered swivel chair.

Alan, a slender, sandy-haired man of average height, strolled over to the sofa placed along the wall facing Reeves's desk. He dropped down and sprawled back comfortably, resting an ankle on his knee.

"Did you catch that match between Becker and Lendl this weekend?" he asked.

"I saw the last set."

The two men briefly discussed the televised final of a major tennis tournament. Anyone overhearing them could easily tell that tennis wasn't a spectator sport for them. They were both avid players and knowledgeable about strategy and technique.

Reeves turned the talk to the practice of law, inquiring, "Did you get a court date on that marine safety violation suit against the tugboat company?" Alan specialized in maritime law.

"Yes, but the case won't go to trial. We'll settle. It was too flagrant a violation of the Coast Guard regulations. Hopefully the tugboat company will straighten up their act." Alan shook his head. "Cases like this one make me sick to my stomach. You wonder how the CEO of this outfit can sleep nights, cutting corners and endangering the lives of his employees. He ought to be put in jail, not just hit in the pocketbook."

Reeves nodded, knowing enough of the details of the case to be completely in accord. His lips tightened as he gestured toward the folder on his desk.

"The same goes for butchers and incompetents in the medical profession, as far as I'm concerned."

Alan eyed him shrewdly. "Another medical malpractice client found his way to your door," he guessed.

"This man isn't able to find his way to my door," Reeves replied grimly. "He isn't walking. He's partially paralyzed with no control over his bladder or bowels. You talk about a horror story. This is one to give you nightmares."

"Surgery patient?"

"Back surgery. Forty-five-year-old man. Blue-collar worker. A welder. Tussling with his teenaged kid in the living room. Just clowning around. Loses his balance and falls and hurts his back. No previous back injuries.

Endures severe pain for several weeks. Finally goes to his family doctor who sends him to our orthopedist-butcher, who carves him up and does permanent nerve damage that ruins him for life."

"Orthopedic surgeon, not neurosurgeon."

"Right. Their training and expertise overlap. My client wasn't hurt on the job. So he's totally disabled without workmen's comp to fall back on."

"And no disability insurance, I take it," Alan put in soberly.

"None. Four kids and a wife whose job skills are being a wife and mother. Plus he requires practical nursing care. It would cost as much as she could earn to hire someone to stay with him while she's at work. Their modest savings account has already been depleted by bills and mortgage payments. They're facing foreclosure on their home and having their car repossessed." Reeves reached for a sheet of scratch paper with numbers on it, crumpled it up into a ball and hurled it into a nearby trash basket.

"Being a bloodsucking, ambulance-chasing, lowlife lawyer, you can't let that happen," Alan suggested dryly. "Even if it means taking on the payments yourself with no guarantee that you'll win the lawsuit and be reimbursed."

"I'll win this lawsuit. The medical evidence is all there, and it's damning. My client will be awarded more money than he could have earned in his lifetime, but it won't be enough. No amount of money can compensate him for what he's lost. His life quality is shot to hell."

"Is the doctor reputable? Could he have just had a bad day in the operating room?"

"It wouldn't surprise me if he needs to join AA," Reeves said. Alan cocked an eyebrow and waited for him to elaborate. "I served him drinks when I bartended at society functions back in my college and law-school years. He's well connected socially. Old New Orleans family. He was a heavy drinker then. I had an opportunity to observe him recently at a charity affair, and he hasn't slacked off."

"A shaky hand with a scalpel. Scary thought." Alan got to his feet. His next words were on another subject. "You haven't come to any decision, I presume?"

Reeves shook his head, easily making the transition. Alan was the only person with whom he'd discussed the offer from Duplantis & Duplantis to join the downtown firm as a junior partner.

"No, I haven't. There're so many pros and cons."

The other attorney strolled to the door, where he stopped to ask, "How about a game of mixed doubles Friday night at the River Center? Kay and I will take on you and her friend Melody." Kay was the woman with whom Alan had had a steady relationship for about a year and a half. She was also his tennis partner in local mixed-doubles tournaments. The River Center was an indoor tennis facility where both men were members. "Remember, you met Melody." Reeves was shaking his head. "Sure you do. She's tall, five-eight or five-nine, short blond hair, blue eyes, Texas accent."

"I remember her. But I'm interested in someone."

Alan blinked. "Friday you were unattached." It was Monday morning. "Who is she? Where did you meet her?"

"Her name is Olivia. Olivia Prescott. I've known her since she was a little girl." Reeves almost absently explained the past connection. Alan was generally familiar with his background.

The sandy-haired man was also keenly observant and a good enough friend to poke good-natured fun. "You look moonstruck, Counselor. I've never seen that expression on your face before."

Reeves grinned sheepishly. "I feel moonstruck. I can't keep my mind off her for more than fifteen minutes."

"Was it mutual? She took one look at you and an unseen symphony started playing celestial music?"

"There's some mutual attraction, all right. But she turned me down flat when I asked her out."

"Smart lady. Got your attention with a swat to the male ego, eh?"

"No, she wasn't playing hard to get."

"Well, if you come down to earth during the next couple of days, let me know. I don't have to tell Kay something definite about the mixed doubles until Wednesday."

With a casual lift of his hand, Alan left. Reeves sat gazing at the empty doorway for a moment. Then he focused on the open file on his desk and sighed.

Damn, why did the doctor in this malpractice suit have to be Dr. Bella? A month ago when he'd taken on the case, it hadn't mattered that Bella was the father of one of Olivia's old girlfriends. Now suddenly it was a cause for regret.

Reeves hadn't remembered Marcia Hymer, but he did recall Sissy Bella. She would have been at the Hymers' dinner party Saturday night if she and her husband hadn't been out of town at a medical convention. The daughter of a physician, she'd married a physician. Olivia's expression had been fond at the mention of Sissy.

When she'd spoken of her old girlfriend, her voice had been warm with affection.

All her loyalties would be with Sissy and the Bellas, no matter how damning the facts of the case were. As the patient's attorney, Reeves would be the villain in her eyes, just as surely as his sister had been the villain in bringing to light the dirty dealings of Olivia's grandfather.

Marcia and Clinton Hymer and their circle of friends would rally around Sissy Bella DeMarco, too. Reeves would definitely be persona non grata when news of the lawsuit came out. The thought of alienating that whole group of new acquaintances, and especially the Hymers, bothered him more than he would ever have expected.

Was it because they were socially prominent people? He preferred to think not. A more palatable explanation was that he'd found the Hymers to be likable people, somewhat to his surprise. He'd been predisposed *not* to find that he had anything in common with them.

Rising abruptly, he walked over to the window overlooking Gravier Street. He could recommend another good attorney to his client. The case hadn't progressed beyond the stage of gathering evidence.

His problem was selling his conscience that solution. It told him, *You took the case, Talbot. You've established an attorney-client relationship. This man and his wife have put their trust in you. They're depending on you.*

A telephone call regarding another case brought him from the window back to his desk. While he was talking to the caller, he closed the folder and put it aside, also postponing any decision for the moment. After he'd hung up, he made a series of calls in the interest of several different clients. When the last phone conversation was concluded, he stood, slipped on his suit jacket and tightened the loosened knot of his tie.

In twenty minutes he had an appointment with a team of high-powered defense attorneys representing a giant supermarket chain. They were ready to talk settlement. Reeves was ready to drive a hard bargain for his client, a woman who'd been fired from her job as checkout clerk because she spurned the advances of her store manager.

His secretary, Joan Shaeffer, was busy at her computer terminal, long, polished nails flashing. She was every bit as efficient and dependable as she was brassy and sharp-spoken. Joan referred to herself as "one more tough broad."

Reeves stopped to confer with her, also to seek some advice. Joan was divorced and single and dated a lot of men.

"A hypothetical situation, Joan. A man asks you out. You turn him down flat. He has it bad and wants to ask you out again. What would be his best tactic?"

She scrutinized him between eyelashes coated with black mascara. "Hmm. If I didn't find the guy too repulsive, his best bet would be to ask me out on a date that was too good to turn down. Say dinner at Commander's Palace and tickets to a Kenny Rogers concert." Joan slapped the air and added cynically, "On second thought, the guy could be repulsive if he had good tickets for front-row reserved seats for a Kenny Rogers concert."

Reeves gave his head a little shake. "I don't think dinner at an expensive restaurant and big-name entertainment would be strong enough enticement," he said regretfully.

"If she has highbrow tastes, she might go for tickets to the opera or the ballet. Women like for a man to go to a lot of expense." Joan shrugged. "Naturally it's all relative as to what is expensive. I read in the paper this morning that patrons' tickets for the Baryshnikov performance are a thousand bucks apiece. Of course, the money goes to charity and for that price you get to meet him at a champagne reception. Personally, I'd rather meet Kenny Rogers."

"That's a charity benefit, isn't it?"

"Yeah, sure, it would be a tax write-off..." Her voice drifted off skeptically.

"Joan, you may just have hit upon the date that will do the trick," Reeves mused. "In any case the money would go to a good cause. Get me a couple of those thousand-dollar tickets."

Her eyebrows shot up to her bleached bangs, but otherwise she was unruffled by the instructions. "If this jerk I'd turned down sent me flowers to soften me up, it could work in his favor," she remarked blandly. "I'm a sucker for roses. Like most women, I have a hard time throwing them in the trash, even if they're red roses."

"What's wrong with red roses?" Reeves asked, his tone defensive.

"They're gorgeous, but they're also the universal choice of men. Roses come in other colors. Pink and yellow and white." Joan smirked. "They usually cost more, since they're less common."

Her words came back to him later in the day as he maneuvered into a parking spot in front of a florist's shop owned and operated by a former client, appropriately named Flo. It was true, he had to admit, that he'd routinely sent red roses to women in the past. There hadn't been a personal element in his choice.

This was the first time he'd actually gone to the trouble to visit a florist and make a selection.

When he left, it was with a credit card receipt for a sum in the hundreds. He had picked out pink roses, the color bringing back an unexpectedly vivid image of Olivia as a little princess of a girl in frilly pink. Flo had inquired whether he wanted an arrangement in a vase. Reeves had said yes, and ended up opting for a crystal vase.

It was a good thing, he reflected to himself with irony, that he'd settled a case and earned a sizable fee today. Dating Olivia was an expensive proposition.

Luckily he could afford it. He could afford *her* now.

What kind of thinking was that? Reeves took himself to task, bothered that such a thought had passed through his mind.

Something was afoot. The intuition grew stronger during lunch at a chic restaurant across from City Park where Marcia had taken Olivia today.

First the lunch date itself had been impromptu. Or *supposedly* impromptu. Marcia had called her last night and made some vague mention of having to be in Metairie around noon. Could Olivia have lunch with her?

The idea of Marcia with a reason to come to Metairie was so unlikely that it had been on the tip of Olivia's tongue to ask what the errand was, but no sooner had she agreed to lunch than Marcia changed the subject. Then she'd cut the conversation short with a plausible, but phony excuse. Olivia could always tell when Marcia wasn't being truthful. Her voice was *too* casual or *too* surprised or *too* apologetic.

Either she had some good news to tell and didn't trust herself not to blab it on the phone or else she'd cooked up some sort of nice surprise for Olivia. Nothing was wrong. Olivia would have sensed that Marcia had bad news.

Then today the plot had thickened. Marcia had picked Olivia up and disclosed when they were out on Veterans' Highway in the thick of traffic that she had lunch reservations at this restaurant, miles away in the city of New Orleans. She'd insisted that it was no problem for her to drive Olivia all the way back to Metairie afterward.

"I have nothing better to do," she'd declared, and airily changed the subject.

Since when had Marcia, as busy as any business executive, had time to play chauffeur? Olivia had sat back, not arguing, but she couldn't resist inquiring with mock innocence, "Will anyone else be joining us?"

"No, it'll just be you and me," Marcia had replied, *too* convincingly.

To Olivia's surprise, at the restaurant they were shown to a table for two. During lunch, Marcia made no special announcement. She produced no gift, asked no favor, made no proposition.

But something was up. Olivia just *knew* it. Finally the suspense got the best of her.

"I'm *dying* of curiosity! When are you going to put me out of my misery and let me in on the secret?" she demanded smilingly while they were waiting for their waiter to return with Marcia's change. She'd insisted that lunch was her treat.

Marcia smiled back nervously. "What on earth are you talking about? You won't be angry with me, promise?" she begged in the next breath. "You know what an incurable romantic I am."

"Marcia! *Tell* me."

Marcia glanced out toward the street with a hint of apprehension. "I'm in collusion with a male admirer of yours."

"What?"

"Oh. Here's my change," she declared, the waiter having returned. Leaving a tip, she scooped up the rest of the bills and stuffed them into her handbag. "Shall we go?"

"Who's the male admirer? How are you 'in collusion' with him?" Olivia pressed for answers as they both got up, preparing to leave.

"I'll explain outside. Just promise me that you'll be a good sport about this."

"About *what?*"

"Well, it's a kidnapping of sorts."

"Marcia, I don't have the afternoon off!" Olivia remonstrated. "I have to get back to work."

"Of course, you do," Marcia soothed.

This conversation took place en route to the restaurant entrance, Marcia leading the way. Out on the sidewalk, she paused. A shiny white Porsche was parked at the curb. The door on the driver's side opened, and a man got out. Intent on getting the promised explanation out of Marcia, Olivia glanced at him and did a surprised double take.

Reeves Talbot.

Marcia greeted him in a friendly manner, and he greeted her cordially. Then he spoke pleasantly to Olivia, coming around his car.

"Hello, Reeves," she said, wondering whether he was meeting a woman for lunch.

To her befuddlement, he opened the passenger's door of the Porsche, revealing a sleek interior with charcoal-gray leather upholstery. Olivia gazed at him blankly and then glanced over at Marcia. At the sight of the latter's guilty smile, she finally put two and two together. *Reeves was the male admirer with whom she was in collusion. He was here to "kidnap" Olivia. This whole lunch date had been cooked up between them.*

"I really don't believe this," Olivia said, sheer disbelief warring with indignation.

"Reeves bribed me with a donation to one of my charities." Marcia made the admission cheerfully. "I didn't think you'd mind doing your part for a good cause. After all, it's not exactly a hardship being transported back to Metairie in a sports car by an attractive man. Is it?"

"What's my alternative? Taking a taxi?"

Marcia wrinkled her nose in apology. "I'm afraid so. I have a committee meeting in thirty minutes."

"I'm as good a driver as my father was," Reeves put in, silencing Olivia with the remark. "I've never had an accident."

He looked as handsome and virile today in a pin-striped suit as he had in his white dinner jacket and dark trousers two weeks ago at Marcia's dinner party. In truth, it *wasn't* a repugnant prospect, riding in his racy, low-slung automobile with him behind the wheel. Quite the opposite.

He wasn't hiding the fact that her daytime appearance met completely with his approval. By coincidence, her new spring suit, an exquisite shade of pink, was the same color as the bouquet of roses that he'd sent her. Olivia was glad that she'd worn the suit, which was becoming.

"You'll take me straight to my job?" she confirmed.

He raised his right hand as though taking a solemn oath in court. "So help me God."

Marcia gave Olivia a little farewell hug. Then with a smile and a wave, she hurried toward her Mercedes, parked several cars away.

Olivia got into the Porsche and fastened her seat belt. The faint scent of leather mingled with the faint masculine scent of his after-shave lotion. She settled back, affecting relaxation, as he slid behind the wheel. It was close quarters, intimate confinement.

"With a car like this one, you shouldn't have to resort to devious methods to give women rides," she remarked.

His seat belt buckled, he started the engine. It purred with leashed power. "Normally I don't resort to such methods. I wasn't confident that I could get you in my car any other way."

He shifted into gear and pulled out into the street. Olivia was on the alert for him to try to take a circuitous route, but he drove at a brisk pace in the direction of Canal Street. Apparently he was heading for the nearest access to Interstate 10.

"What did you have for lunch?" he inquired, braking for a red light. "I hear the food is good there."

"I had trout amandine, and it was delicious. I recommend that you try the restaurant yourself."

He smiled at her and coaxed lightly, "Don't I get any small talk in the bargain?"

"I didn't strike any bargain with you, Reeves. The deal was between you and Marcia. I'm simply making the best of being put in an untenable position."

The light turned green, and he accelerated, the car responding with a smooth, forward surge.

"It's almost pleasure enough to look at you, without carrying on conversation." The words of flattery were spoken with a rueful sincerity that she found hard to resist. "Actually I was half hoping that you weren't so lovely in the light of day. Most women look better at night, but that's not true of you."

"I could return the compliment," she said, treating herself to a glance over at him. She wished that he weren't so clean-cut and good-looking in the light of day, so vital, so personable. So virile. It would be much easier to discourage him if she didn't find him so attractive.

"Then we both like each other's looks. That's enough basis for at least one date, isn't it?" he urged.

"It would be, if we were strangers. But we aren't. We know each other too well."

"I disagree. We don't know each other well. And I want to get to know you better."

"Do you? Or is your ego just hurt because a woman turned you down?" It wasn't a taunt, but he winced at her directness.

"All indications to the contrary, I don't have a problem taking no from a woman. If you go out with me and don't want to repeat the experience, I won't argue or persist. I give you my word on that. And my word is good," he added.

"There's absolutely *no* chance that I would want to become involved in a dating relationship with you, Reeves. In *any* kind of relationship. There's too much bad feeling between us, too many painful memories."

"There's also now and the fact that we're attracted to each other."

Olivia didn't bother to make a denial. Her acquiescence didn't change anything. Reeves was still Doreen's sister. His place of residence was still Olivia's old home.

The light at the Canal Street intersection was green, and they sped through, two of New Orleans's historic cemeteries over on the left and another on the right with above-the-ground tombs and monuments. Moments later he was merging his low-slung sports car with fast-moving traffic on the interstate.

"Your suit is the same pink as the roses I sent you," he commented. "I hope that means that you liked my choice."

"You saw them?" Olivia blurted out in her surprise.

"I went to the florist and personally picked them out. You wore pink a lot as a little girl. The color kind of struck a sentimental chord."

"Of course I liked them," she said, not wanting to pursue that line of conversation. "They were beautiful. I took them to work so that my co-workers could enjoy them, too."

His quick glance was perceptive. "Did you put them on your desk?"

"No," she answered truthfully. "May I return the Waterford vase to you?"

"You don't like Waterford?" His question seemed to convey uncertainty over whether he'd chosen well.

"Yes, I like Waterford. But I also know how expensive it is." Was he typically that extravagant, sending flowers in a crystal vase? she wondered, but didn't ask.

Disconcertingly, he read her mind and was put on the defensive. "I don't ordinarily throw my money around and play the big spender, if that's what you're thinking."

"I'm sorry you've gone to such expense for nothing. Between your florist's bill and your donation to Marcia's charity, you're out of pocket for quite a bit of money, I gather. But evidently you're a very successful attorney and can afford it."

He changed lanes. "Fortunately, I can even afford the two tickets for the Baryshnikov benefit performance that I bought to try to lure you into going out with me. They're patrons' tickets and cost a grand apiece." He smiled a wry smile. "At this rate, I may turn into a philanthropist."

She stared at him accusingly. "You have patrons' tickets to the Baryshnikov performance? That was the date you had in mind? Attending the Baryshnikov performance?" Olivia's tone was faintly reproachful. How could he have guessed that she would dearly love to see Baryshnikov dance? She'd even tried to get tickets, not patrons' tickets, of course.

"The date I *have* in mind," he admitted. "I haven't given up yet. Can't I entice you to go with me? According to my secretary, the seats are close enough to the stage to see the weave of his leotard. Marcia and Clinton have patrons' tickets, too."

"I know they do. Marcia mentioned it at lunch."

"There'll be a champagne reception afterward that Baryshnikov will attend. I suspect that New Orleans society will be out in force."

He plainly assumed that that information would serve as an inducement. Olivia wanted to set him straight.

"Without doubt. But the main draw for me would be the actual performance, not seeing and being seen. This is really very underhanded of you, Reeves, dangling an invitation that I would find so difficult to refuse."

"Don't refuse." He pressed on. "It's only one evening of my company. If you don't want to go out with me again, I won't bother you."

"This will be our *only* date. If you can't accept that, I would advise you to make better use of those tickets and invite someone else to go with you."

"There isn't any other woman I want to invite."

He was obviously as deeply pleased over the success of his strategy as Olivia was filled with strong misgivings. She resented him for having manipulated her so easily without any regard to what was best for her. Under the charm was a ruthless man she didn't dare like or trust.

"How *is* Doreen these days?" she asked him. "I know she works for Channel 4 news." Olivia was careful never to tune in the news on that station.

Reeves didn't answer at once. "As far as I know, she's fine. We don't see each other very often."

"She doesn't visit you at your condominium?"

Her taut question drew a sharp glance, but he answered evenly. "No, as a matter of fact, she hasn't visited me once since I moved there a year ago. I doubt that she's likely to. My address is as offensive to her as it is to you." He lifted a hand from the wheel in a gesture that was both impatient and imploring. "Look, I really wasn't satisfying any psychological hang-ups by buying my condo. It was a great real-estate deal at the time, and I needed the tax write-off for a home mortgage. The possibility never occurred to me that I'd meet you and—" He broke off not finishing.

"Here's our exit," Olivia said.

"Do you believe me?"

"I can believe that you might not have consciously been getting your revenge on my grandparents—and on me—when you moved into the Prescott mansion. But if you're honest with yourself, I think you'll admit that there was some deeper significance to owning that particular real estate.''

''I don't know about 'deeper significance,''' Reeves protested. ''I will admit that I was a little intrigued by the notion of having partial ownership in the old Prescott mansion.''

''Just like you're a little intrigued by the notion of dating Olivia Prescott, former spoiled brat and debutante?''

''Come on!'' His objection was angry. ''I would want to date you no matter who you were. You're beautiful and intelligent and sexy in a classy kind of way that appeals to me.''

''No man has ever gone to as much trouble and expense as you have to get a date with me. Have *you* ever gone to this trouble and expense before?''

''No,'' he conceded, his frown saying clearly that he didn't like her theory at all.

''You should get in the right lane,'' she suggested. ''The office building where I work is in the next block.''

They rode in tense silence.

''I'll call you and get directions to your apartment,'' Reeves said when he'd pulled up in front of the entrance and braked.

Olivia was reaching to open the door. ''It's not necessary for you to pick me up. I'll meet you at the Theatre of the Performing Arts. That is, unless you've changed your mind and want to take back your invitation.''

He ignored the last. ''I would prefer to pick you up.''

She objected. ''That's an old-fashioned attitude.''

"Maybe it is, but I still wouldn't feel easy sending you home in your car late at night. Besides, I want my full quota of time spent in your company."

"Very well."

Evidently he had changed his mind about dating her, but through some stubbornness was refusing to break this one and only date. By dissecting his interest in her, Olivia must have killed it.

She told herself with a little inner despondent sigh that she certainly hoped she'd discouraged him.

Chapter Three

Olivia dabbed perfume on her neck and wrists and was ready with five minutes to spare. Tonight her fashion statement was "sparkle and shine."

No black silk dress and demure pearls for her tonight. No poor, but proud demeanor. She'd thrown economy to the winds when she went on her shopping spree for an outfit for tonight. Her beaded white gown and faux-ruby-and-diamond earrings had made a huge dent in her bank account, but it felt wonderful, for a change, to splurge. Who cared if she ended up making a donation of dress and jewelry to the Junior League?

"My God! You look like a celebrity!" Judy gasped, her blue eyes widening with awe, when Olivia came out of her bedroom. "That dress is *gorgeous* on you! I'm glad you didn't do your hair a different way. It's so natural looking and yet sophisticated. Nature gave you a soft perm." She flipped a lock of her own fine blond hair which she regularly had permed for body.

Olivia had toyed with the idea of pinning her hair up in a more sleek hairdo, but instead she'd gone with Judy's advice and just blow-dried her hair as usual. A couple of inches shy of shoulder-length, it was styled to encourage its natural tendency to curl and wave, the overall effect mussed and yet chic.

"There he is." Judy cocked her head toward the sound of the door chimes. "You have to invite him in to meet me, since, according to you, this is your first and last date with him. If he's really as good-looking as that newspaper picture, I may ask him to pose for a snapshot for my album."

"The newspaper picture didn't flatter him." Olivia was on her way toward their small foyer, walking with a light tread in her white silk pumps. With her hand on the knob, she paused just a second and then opened the door.

Reeves stood there, tall and urbane in tuxedo and black tie. His lips parted, but no words came out. He closed them without speaking, gazing at her in mute admiration. Olivia's smile died away, her pulse quickening as she exchanged wordless compliments with him.

You look incredibly beautiful.

You look incredibly handsome.

Her smile bloomed again on her lips to the sound of his deep audible breath. "You're right on time," she said.

"Ready?" he asked.

Olivia didn't remember Judy, waiting in the living room, until she was getting into his racy white Porsche.

While he was walking around to the driver's side, she settled herself against the leather upholstery of her seat.

It was supple and smooth, enveloping her in luxury. Inhaling, she drew in the clean masculine scent of well-groomed man.

Then he was sliding under the wheel. The dusky interior of the car seemed more intimate by night. His virility was an even stronger component of his physical presence than it had been in the daylight. He turned the key in the ignition and the engine leapt to life, humming a powerful accompaniment to classical music that swelled from the car speakers with marvelous clarity.

"No, don't turn it down," Olivia requested as he moved his hand toward the lighted stereo panel. Her pleasure was in her voice. "That's absolutely wonderful sound."

He dropped his hand instead to the stick shift. "Are you comfortable?" he asked, looking at her inquiringly as though trying to determine the answer for himself. "I considered renting a larger car for tonight."

"I'm very comfortable," she assured him. In her self-indulgent mood, it seemed okay to add, "I adore your car. I would have been disappointed if you'd shown up in a rented car."

"You do like it?" He appeared and sounded inordinately pleased.

"If I won a sports car in a sweepstakes, I would want it to be a Porsche. And that's my best chance of owning one," she added gaily.

He shifted into gear. "Maybe it's your best chance as a single woman. You're so damned beautiful that you could marry a rich man and have a garage full of Porsches." It was a fervent statement, not lightly flattering.

"I don't run into too many rich men out here in Metairie," Olivia pointed out. "But, thank you for the compliment."

The music, which had gotten softer during a movement with violins, swelled louder as the full orchestra joined in. Olivia and Reeves dispensed with talking in favor of listening. He pulled out of the parking lot of the apartment complex. Minutes later they were speeding along the interstate.

Following a rousing crescendo, marking the end of the symphony by Beethoven, a radio announcer came on. Reeves turned the volume low.

"How is it that you've managed to stay single anyway?" he asked.

"Easy. I haven't said 'yes' to a proposal of marriage."

"You must have had at least a dozen of those, I'm sure."

"Not that many," she denied. "But a few. What about you? You're five years older than I am, and you're still single. That tells me you haven't proposed to a woman."

He shrugged. "Up to now I've been too busy to even think about settling down, what with college, law school and then establishing a law practice. I had student loans to pay off."

"I had to pay off a student loan, too," Olivia said. "I had to borrow money to finish college."

He wasn't to be sidetracked from her unmarried status. "You haven't let a guy put an engagement ring on your finger?"

"Actually I have been engaged twice," she admitted. Three times if she counted her unofficial engagement to William Duplantis. But she didn't want to bring him up or think about that terribly unhappy period of her life. "Both times I didn't wear the ring very long. I got cold feet. Marriage is such a scary prospect. We have so much evidence these days with the divorce statistics that love doesn't conquer all." Her tone was light, suggesting that they probably didn't want to get into heavy discussions tonight.

"So you've been in love with two different men?"

"Not in the 'head-over-heels-in-love' tradition, but I cared for both men in a deep, affectionate way or I wouldn't have considered marrying them."

"They fell for you hard and pressured you to marry them," he guessed.

"Men get in a marrying state of mind," Olivia said evasively. His analysis was unerring. "Sam and Eric both have found wives more suitable than I was. I wouldn't have made either one of them a good wife. Fortunately for them, I realized that, if they didn't."

"What made you come to that realization? Was there some similarity in the two sets of circumstances?"

She smiled her reproval for his inquisitiveness. "Aren't you being a little personal, Mr. Attorney?"

"It doesn't seem to be a painful subject," Reeves was quick to point out.

"Aren't you supposed to withdraw your questions, since I've raised an objection to your line of questioning?" Playfully she used courtroom terminology.

"Only if the objection is sustained. Would you mind telling me? It's not idle curiosity. I'm thinking that it might be good for me to hear."

Olivia sighed. "Yes, I suppose there was a similarity. In both instances, I woke up to reality when I was introduced to my future in-laws and family members."

"Sam and Eric were both from middle-class back-grounds?"

"Background had nothing to do with it," she pro-tested, seeing the direction of his thoughts. "There wasn't any snobbery involved. I just wasn't enough in love with either man."

She could sense that she hadn't really convinced him.

"So you've never been in love?" he asked.

"Not as an adult. Have you?"

"Lots of times, but it never lasted."

Olivia shook her head. "You men. Your emotions don't run very deep." Immediately she regretted the words, feeling his glance probe her face. "Now shall we lighten up the conversation and just enjoy the eve-ning?"

Another musical selection had begun playing on the radio, a turbulent piece. Reeves turned up the volume. The passion and emotion in the music filled the car, like troubling, revealing dialogue of the senses between them.

It was a relief to arrive at the theater, where the park-ing lot was filling up with Lincolns and Cadillacs and Mercedes. Here and there a Rolls-Royce could be spot-ted. Olivia saw at once that she and Reeves weren't overdressed for the occasion. Men in formal wear es-corted beautifully dressed women toward the theater entrance. Glamour was definitely the keynote. Social stimulation was in the air, as heady as champagne.

Inside the lobby, with its splendid modern chandelier setting the tone of elegance, they encountered Marcia and Clinton Hymer. Marcia was radiant in red lace and a rope of pearls. Clinton looked like a distinguished teddy bear in his black tux. After hugs and handshakes of greeting, the four of them went together to the lobby bar.

It was a slow journey because every few steps they had to stop to say hello to friends and acquaintances. Olivia came in for raving compliments and got a lion's share of attention. She put aside old hurts and hard-won insights and smiled and played her role easily, with surprisingly little strain. This was only a visit back into her old world, but she could allow herself to enjoy the whole familiar ambiance.

Reeves responded pleasantly to introductions and seemed at ease. If he would rather have had her to himself, he didn't show it. Apparently he was content to mingle and participate in the social interacting, which was as superficial as Olivia remembered it, with real attitudes and opinions cloaked in politeness.

As the lobby grew more crowded, she was jostled a time or two. Reeves drew her closer to shield her with his body, giving her a nice feeling of being protected. The touch of his hand at her waist was not intimate or possessive, but that of a courteous escort. But when she smiled up at him, he squeezed briefly. A warm sexy tingle spread through her from the point of contact.

"Shall we find our seats?" she suggested, wanting to escape the close quarters.

Her haze of pleasure subsided to a comfortable level as she accompanied him inside the theater down near the stage to their choice reserved seats. Their immediate neighbors, strangers to Olivia, were already seated so that the two empty seats formed a little oasis that seemed dauntingly private.

"With a little forethought, I might have gotten seats next to the Hymers," Reeves said.

"Yes, that would have been nice," Olivia replied, irked at herself for her own insincerity and at him for wanting to continue the socializing. She *didn't* really regret not sitting next to the Hymers. "However, I'm just as glad not to have distractions. I'm really looking forward to seeing Baryshnikov."

He'd taken only one program for them to share. She opened it and held it so that he could look at it with her. He shifted his body so that his shoulder rested lightly against hers.

"Can you see well enough?" she inquired.

He smiled at her. "Quite frankly, that program isn't fascinating reading for me. I'm just taking advantage of the opportunity to sit close."

"You're not a ballet fan."

"Not up to this point in my life. This is my first ballet performance."

"It sounds as though you don't think that it will be your last."

He shrugged, causing his shoulder to rub against hers, the smooth fabric of his black tux sliding against the luminous white beading of her dress. "I'm open to developing some cultural appreciation."

What was behind this sudden openness? Olivia didn't have to ask. She could provide the answer for herself. Cultural appreciation went hand in hand with social prominence. Reeves would attend the ballet and the opera and the symphony to rub elbows with people like the Hymers.

The lights lowered, a hush fell and music heralded the beginning of the much-awaited performance. Along with the rest of the audience, Olivia drew in her breath as floodlights dramatically lit the set of a fantasyland forest and dancers leapt from the wings.

She focused her eyes upon the stage in rapt appreciation as the highly professional production unfolded, showcasing Baryshnikov, who lived up to all of Olivia's expectations.

"Isn't he marvelous?" she murmured in Reeves's ear at the end of a number, amidst enthusiastic applause. She and Reeves were both clapping.

He had bent his head to catch her remark. Nodding, he shifted his body lower in his seat. When he turned his head to speak a low reply to her, their faces were mere inches apart.

"The man's quite an athlete," he said. "I'm impressed."

But the admiring light in his dark eyes seemed to be all for her. Olivia's breath caught in her throat as she looked back at him.

"It's a thrill of a lifetime to see him dance in person," she declared.

A wry smile lifted one corner of his mouth. "I won't go that far."

The smile faded as he dropped his gaze to her lips. Olivia felt a jolting sensation in the pit of her stomach. She was suddenly short of air, and evidently he was, too, because he inhaled sharply. They looked into each other's eyes, carrying on a primal communication, Baryshnikov forgotten. The only topic between them was his urge to kiss her and her urge to let him.

The clapping had died down, and the next number was beginning. Olivia forced her attention back to the stage, shaken by her desire to feel his lips on hers.

Surely what had just happened was an effect of the wonderful performance, but she'd gotten a clear reading on how potent the attraction was between her and

Reeves. It could easily flame out of control, out of *his* control as well as hers.

At intermission he stood and seemed eager to join the mass exodus for the lobby. Evidently he was ready for more socializing. Taking his arm, Olivia went along, dreading the crush. For her part, she would have been content to stay in her seat.

They obviously made a striking couple judging from the second glances directed at them. She noted with some amusement that the male consensus deemed Reeves a lucky man to have her draped on his arm, while female consensus voted her as the lucky one of the pair.

"What's funny?" Reeves asked curiously as they stepped out into the lobby. Olivia didn't get a chance to answer, because at that moment Sissy DeMarco shrieked out her name in a delighted tone.

"Olivia!"

"Sissy!"

Olivia released Reeves's arm to give Sissy a warm hug that was just as warmly returned. "It's so good to see you, Sissy!"

"It's good to see you! I was so mad that I missed you at Marcia's dinner party a couple of weeks ago. You look *gorgeous!* I'm so jealous—look at my husband, all smiles, waiting for his hug and kiss!"

Olivia turned to George DeMarco, Sissy's physician husband, who made a great show of smacking her on the cheek. He was a short, stocky, balding man in his early forties. There was a fourteen-year difference in age between him and Sissy, who, Olivia knew, had anything but a reason to be jealous. George adored his wife.

The DeMarcos both looked expectantly at Reeves, waiting for Olivia to introduce him. She glanced smilingly at his face and felt her smile falter at the sudden change in him. His manner had grown stiff and formal. His expression was aloof.

What had caused the change?

"Reeves Talbot." He identified himself during the few seconds of awkwardness. George DeMarco proffered his hand, and Reeves shook hands with him formally.

"You look familiar, Reeves," Sissy mused, cocking her head to one side and regarding him with blinking concentration. "Don't I know you?"

"I'm a local attorney," he replied. "Recently I think I saw you at a fund-raiser for Children's Hospital."

"Yes, I *was* there...."

"I see that your mother and father are here, Sissy. How nice. I'll get to say hello to them." Olivia had spotted Dr. and Mrs. Bella heading their way. She spoke up to focus attention on them and sidetrack Sissy from her attempt to place Reeves.

The older couple joined them, and there was pleasant confusion, at least pleasant on Olivia's part. She had always been fond of Sissy's parents. They'd been kinder to her than any of the other parents of girlfriends when Olivia had lost her grandparents, lost *everything*. They'd even offered her a home, which she'd refused.

"Reeves, I want you to meet two of the nicest people in the world," she said with deep affection, introducing him.

If possible, his manner was even more frigid than a few minutes earlier. Olivia was mystified. Why was he so standoffish with Sissy and George and with the Bellas? Had some incident occurred in the past causing dislike of the Bella family? That was the only explanation that seemed plausible, and yet the Bellas weren't at all the type of people to be high-handed with domestic help.

"Shall we avoid the crush and go back to our seats?" Olivia suggested to him with a smile when it was politely possible to break away. Another mature couple had come up to greet Dr. and Mrs. Bella, providing the opportunity.

"We'll get together soon," Sissy promised Olivia warmly in parting. She smiled and added in a stage whisper, "I plan to call you tomorrow and give you the third degree about this divinely handsome attorney you're dating." Her tone changed to normal. "Maybe by then I'll figure out why he looks so familiar."

Olivia didn't slip her arm inside Reeves's arm as she accompanied him back inside the theater. His expression and his bearing didn't encourage her to take any liberties. The touch of his hand at the small of her back was impersonal. Encountering the DeMarcos and the Bellas had definitely brought about a transformation in him, one that she wanted explained to her.

"If Sissy calls, shall I solve the mystery for her?" she asked when they were seated.

"That's entirely up to you what you tell Sissy about me," he replied.

"No, it isn't up to me. It's your background and your privacy involved, not mine."

"If you're not embarrassed, then tell her I was the bartender she asked repeatedly to dance with her at your sixteenth birthday party."

"That's right. Sissy hung around you all night. She ignored her date." Olivia made a little grimace. "But then we all ignored our dates that night, feeding your ego, didn't we? I threw myself at you and, as usual, you couldn't be bothered to be nice to me."

"I handled the situation without much sensitivity," Reeves admitted. "I felt bad afterward."

Olivia went on in self-derision. "I was guided by some silly romantic notion that I could sweep you off your feet if I could just get you to put your arms around me and touch your lips to mine. I thought that a kiss would melt away all your dislike and make you my admiring slave."

"And then what?" Reeves asked. "What came next after I'd become your admiring slave?"

"I don't know," she admitted honestly. "I never got that far. I was only sixteen years old at the time. Would it have hurt you to give me a little peck on the lips? It was my birthday."

"I've already said that I overreacted."

He brought them back to the subject of disclosing his background. "Tell Sissy whatever you like. I would have told her just now why I looked familiar except for starting a discussion that you might find very uncomfortable."

"Was that why you acted so unfriendly?" Olivia inquired. "You felt as though you were being put in an awkward position?"

"That was partly the problem." He hesitated. "Also, I handle some medical malpractice cases in my law practice."

"Oh. So you were ill at ease because George and Dr. Bella are both doctors. Suing physicians and hospitals is very common these days, isn't it? According to Sissy, that's why doctors have to carry so much malpractice insurance, raising the cost of medical care."

"Unfortunately, a medical degree doesn't guarantee competence. A physician's error or the wrong treatment by a hospital staff member can drastically alter a patient's quality of life, not to mention cause death."

"But a doctor or a nurse or an orderly, no matter how skilled and well trained, is still a human being. Medicine isn't an exact science. The doctors I know personally are conscientious and devoted to treating illness and saving lives. Dr. Bella, for example. I would trust myself to his care with complete confidence knowing he's a wonderful human being as well as a highly respected physician."

Reeves made a choking sound and abruptly wiped his hand across his mouth.

"Are you handling a medical malpractice case now?" Olivia asked, struck by some intuition.

He gave her a brief nod. "As a matter of fact, I am."

The theater was filling up. He stood to let a couple pass. When he sat down again, he picked up the program from her lap and opened it, obviously preferring to drop the subject.

Olivia didn't want to know any details of his medical malpractice case anyway. She was just as glad not to discuss his law practice because her bias against plaintiff attorneys in general might come out and would offend him.

The second half of the performance began, but somehow Olivia couldn't immerse herself in the dance and the music as she had done during the first half. She was conscious that Reeves seemed more deep in thought than attentive as he fixed his eyes on the stage. Was his mind still on the scene with the DeMarcos and the Bellas? she wondered.

Fortunately, neither couple was attending the champagne reception for holders of patrons' tickets, so there wouldn't be another encounter.

The reception was at a hotel in the French Quarter. Reeves seemed entirely at ease once again as he and Olivia met up with Marcia and Clinton Hymer. Conversation was mostly about the performance.

Baryshnikov made his appearance. Everyone present got to meet him, as promised, and compliment him in person. Meanwhile, a photographer with the *Times-Picayune* had arrived to take photos, and there was even a photographer with a Minicam shooting footage for the local TV channels. It seemed to Olivia that one or the other of the cameras was pointed at her most of the time. She had to conquer the urge to turn her back and avoid being photographed.

"Is something wrong?" Reeves inquired, speaking the words close to her ear.

Before Olivia could murmur a reply, a male voice close behind her spoke his name in an extremely cordial tone. She could feel her smile freeze into place and her body stiffen. Reeves's gaze lingered on her face a moment before he responded to the greeting from William Duplantis III, her ex-fiancé.

She had glimpsed William and his wife, Debra Sue, earlier and was prepared to speak to them at some point during the reception. It simply came as an unpleasant shock for him to suddenly be there, so near, without any warning. For just a moment, all the shame, the grief, the despair, the sense of total devastation that had also taken her unawares years ago came flooding back.

She had gotten through it.

Olivia's pride in herself, which had no relation to haughtiness, came to her rescue now. With poise restored, she turned around to greet William and Debra Sue. Still, she was grateful that Reeves, apparently sensing that she could use some moral support, circled her waist with his arm and held her close beside him.

He also carried the conversation, much as she had earlier at the theater with the DeMarcos and the Bellas. Debra Sue Duplantis, a petite blond woman, kept a bright smile on her face and let William do most of the talking.

Olivia could deduce for herself that the Duplantises, having to decide between avoiding her and seeking out Reeves, had opted for the latter. There seemed to be a male rapport between the two men. William was not only cordial toward Reeves, but admiring.

Was the rumor true that Marcia had heard? she wondered. Was William's old family law firm actually considering extending an offer to Reeves to join the firm?

As a member of Duplantis & Duplantis, he could realize his social ambitions, especially if he married a Debra Sue, from old money.

Olivia's morale suddenly fell rock bottom. She was ready to have the evening end and go back to Metairie.

Chapter Four

"William Duplantis! Just the man I need to ask a big favor of!"

Marcia Hymer, with her husband in tow, made a timely interruption. Reeves suspected that she had come to the rescue.

Keeping his arm around Olivia's waist, he steered them to a spot some distance away, out of earshot of the group they'd left.

"Are you okay?" he inquired, trying to sound solicitous rather than fiercely protective.

"I could have *died* just now," she murmured.

"I could tell," he said.

The newspaper photographer had come up and requested that he and Olivia and Duplantis and his wife turn and pose for the camera. He'd sensed that the other three were all mortified. The reason wasn't clear to him, but he could guess that it had something to do with an old romance between Olivia and Duplantis.

"William's wife looked like she wished she could sink through the floor," he remarked.

"I'm sure."

There was no rancor or jealousy that he could detect at the mention of Debra Sue Duplantis.

"If it's all the same with you, I've had enough," Olivia said apologetically.

"Why don't we go somewhere and get some real food?" Fancy canapés were being served along with champagne.

"I'm really not hungry. Are you?"

Reeves wasn't hungry, but he wanted to prolong the evening. "Actually I'm starving," he lied. "We can invite the Hymers." It was a halfhearted offer.

She sighed. "No, let's don't. Let's go somewhere where we won't run into everyone here."

Where they wouldn't run into Duplantis was what she meant, of course. It had obviously been very painful for her to be in his company. The reflection brought a sharp stab of jealousy to Reeves's breast.

He took her to a restaurant/bar in one of the big luxury hotels on Canal Street. It was noisier than he would have liked, but wasn't patronized by the uptown crowd who had attended the Baryshnikov performance.

Heads turned and eyes followed them as they made their way to a table, but not because Reeves was wearing a tux and Olivia was dressed to the nines. There were other men in formal wear and women in evening outfits and splashy jewelry. But none of those women, he was sure, had the inbred elegance and indefinable touch of class that Olivia had.

Reeves was proud, as he had been all evening, that she was with him.

"Every guy in the place is envying me," he remarked after they'd sat down.

"Every woman is envying me." But her next words revealed that her mind was on Duplantis, not him. "You and William seem to be very friendly. Does he *know* about you?" she asked.

Reeves took a moment before answering, as though he were making the mental transition. "He knows that I have a law degree from Loyola and that when he opposes me in court, he has his work cut out for him." Reeves had come out the winner so far in those contests. "Those are the primary facts that interest him about me, I assume. Although I wouldn't be surprised if he hadn't delved into my background."

"I'll bet he has," Olivia reflected. "I can still read him. He had trouble hiding how surprised he was over the fact that you and I were out together."

The conversation was interrupted briefly as a waitress in skimpy black attire with a top hat on her head delivered menus and took their drink order. She flounced off after they'd both requested coffee.

"I gather that Duplantis is an old boyfriend of yours," Reeves said, putting aside his menu. He was familiar with its offerings.

Olivia opened hers and scanned it as she replied. "William was more than an old boyfriend. He was my fiancé at the time that my grandfather ended his life. Our engagement hadn't been officially announced, but everyone knew."

Everyone who counted in her world, not people of no consequence, like Reeves, who obviously hadn't known.

There was no intended slight, but the slight was there, nevertheless.

"He broke it off?"

"No, I broke it off. He let me. Oh, he protested his undying love and willingness to marry me anyway. No doubt he would have done the honorable thing, if I'd held him to it. I didn't."

"Are you still—do you..." Reeves's question stuck in his throat.

Olivia shook her head. "No, I'm not still carrying the torch for William. Debra Sue is more than welcome to him."

She didn't sound bitter, just faintly contemptuous. Reeves was disturbed by how much he wanted to believe her.

"Then why was it so traumatic for you to run into him?" he asked.

"It *was* more traumatic than I would have expected," she admitted, continuing to study the food selections. "But probably also therapeutic. I hadn't realized that I still must have some hurt and disappointment bottled up inside of me." She closed her menu. "I'll have a cup of turtle soup and the shrimp remoulade."

The waitress came to serve their coffee, took their food order and departed again. Reeves was formulating a question he really didn't want to ask.

"Maybe you have some hidden regrets about not holding Duplantis to his word?"

She shook her head. "No, I really don't think I do."

"If you'd gone ahead and married him, you'd be living in the Garden District, enjoying the benefits of being Mrs. William Duplantis III." Reeves took a big swallow of black coffee, scalding his mouth.

"It's all water under the bridge now," she said. "I don't live in the Garden District. I live in Metairie, and I'm quite happy." Her wan tone belied her words.

"You must miss being a part of the social scene. Tonight you were in your element."

"Maybe it *seemed* that I was in my element. Social skills may get a little rusty, but you don't lose them."

Once again she obviously hadn't meant to insult him by implying that he'd been taken in because he *wasn't* in his element, coming from a lower-class background. The insult was there though.

"There's a nosy question that I'd like to ask you," she said. "Is the rumor true that you may be getting an offer to join Duplantis & Duplantis?"

"It isn't true that I 'may' be getting an offer. Duplantis & Duplantis has approached me with an offer."

"I'm very pleased for you. That tells me that you must be a good attorney in your own right."

"I am a good attorney. But I was pleased to get the offer," he admitted.

"You're going to take it, I assume. It's more than a career opportunity, as I'm sure you realize. It's a chance to make good social contacts. You could end up a member of an old exclusive Mardi Gras *krewe* like Rex someday. If you have a daughter, she could be a debutante."

And his wife, the mother of the daughter-debutante, might possibly be honored to be Mrs. Reeves Talbot, a moniker that didn't carry a lot of social perks at the present time.

Their food was served. Reeves forced himself to eat, as though nourishment might heal his battered ego.

He hadn't decided to take the offer from Duplantis &
Duplantis, as she assumed. At the moment he had never
been more undecided.

Before tonight, he had seemed to be giving up more
than he was gaining. He liked being his own boss, taking on cases that interested him and turning down those
that didn't. He was free to do *pro bono* work and ad-
just his fees. It was important to him that ordinary people could be represented by an excellent attorney, not
have to settle for poor legal representation.

Olivia's very presence seemed to put all those priori-
ties in question.

They didn't linger at the restaurant. It was obvious
that the evening had worn down to a disappointing con-
clusion for both of them.

"Would you like to go somewhere else?" Reeves made
the perfunctory inquiry in the car.

Olivia declined politely. "No, it's late."

They drove up Canal Street, with its aura of tawdry
elegance. Once the high-class center of shopping in New
Orleans, it had been deserted by the luxury department
stores and upscale retail establishments, who'd moved to
suburban shopping centers. Neon letters flashed on and
off in the windows of pawn shops protected by heavy
grilles. Garish banners announcing huge discounts on
merchandise decorated the storefronts of cheap department stores. Titles of current movies were spelled out on
the marquees of a few old-fashioned movie theaters.

In the mood he was in now, the gritty atmosphere ap-
pealed to Reeves. Those poorly dressed people in evidence on the sidewalks, members of the inner city
population, could well be some of his clients.

Speeding along the interstate, Olivia broke the silence, remarking whimsically, "I could ride all night in

your car, listening to music like this, just travel on and on with no destination."

"Eventually we'd get tired and have to check into a motel," Reeves replied.

She didn't answer.

The sense of dull anticlimax was suddenly gone, replaced by awareness. Reeves looked over at her, and she returned the look. Warmth spread through his long body.

"I wasn't being suggestive," she protested.

"I didn't think you were. You probably mean to get rid of me with a handshake and a thank-you speech when we reach your apartment."

"Actually my thoughts hadn't gotten that far. Going on past experience, I wouldn't have the nerve to offer you a good-night kiss."

"You're not sixteen anymore," Reeves answered.

"Well, considering how expensive a date I've been, you deserve to take your choice of a handshake and a good-night kiss."

"If I were smart, I would take the handshake." But he wouldn't.

"Why is that?" She second-guessed the answer with her next question. "Has our date tonight cured you of the attraction?"

"It's made me wary of the attraction. I have the feeling that I'm getting in over my head." Had *gotten* in over his head was more like it. "Also, I don't know where I stand with you."

"Nothing has changed my original point of view. We're not suited for each other. I'm wrong for you, and you're wrong for me."

The regret in her voice helped salve his wounded feelings a little, but not much.

"That's pretty much the way I see it, too. Our backgrounds are against us."

She nodded. "And our values aren't the same."

What did she know about his values just based on tonight? What did she know about who he was and what made him tick? Apparently as much as she wanted to know.

There seemed nothing more to say. All that remained was the good-night kiss and saying goodbye.

At her apartment building, Reeves switched off the ignition, turning off the car stereo as well as the engine. His fingers tightened on the cold metal of the key as he wrestled with the temptation to turn the stereo back on and have music playing while he kissed her.

"No, don't." Olivia had read his mind.

He dropped his hand and turned sideways toward her. She shifted sideways in her seat, very carefully. "I hope I don't scratch your beautiful leather upholstery with my beaded dress," she said.

"It's a dynamite dress. You look very glamorous in it. Very sexy," he added, paying her compliments he had been paying with his eyes all night.

The glittery white beaded fabric, not pleasant to the touch, sheathed her slim curves like seductive armor. It was the kind of dress that teased a man's imagination, made him want to slide down the zipper and peel the dress off, exposing silky undergarments and soft skin underneath. Under different circumstances Reeves would have told her all that, too.

"Thank you. It was very impractical of me to buy it. But I'm not sorry. I enjoyed wearing it tonight. I would buy it all over again." She touched one hand to the lobe of an ear. "And these designer earrings, too."

"You're not sorry?" Reeves was asking about more than buyer's remorse over an extravagant purchase.

"I wouldn't have missed seeing Baryshnikov dance for anything. It was marvelous attending the performance and having wonderful seats. You were a perfect escort. I enjoyed seeing the Hymers and the DeMarcos. And for the rest of my life, I can say that Baryshnikov kissed my hand." She smiled at him. "Thank you for an enjoyable evening."

"Enjoyable up to a point, you mean. After we ran into Duplantis it was downhill from there, wasn't it?"

Olivia lifted one hand in a graceful gesture. "That part of the evening was memorable, to say the least. Life can't all be good entertainment. I try to remember the good and block out the rest."

"If I could block out anything about tonight, I would block out the good and focus on the bad. About the best that I can hope for is that the good and bad will cancel each other out."

"Well, good night. And goodbye. I wish you every success in your career move."

She leaned toward him and Reeves leaned toward her. Their faces about a foot apart, they stopped. Olivia closed her eyes and drew in a breath. She tipped her head slightly back, making her lips more accessible.

"Somehow this seems familiar," she murmured.

"Too familiar." Reeves's voice came out husky. "If I had any sense, you know, I would kiss you hard like I did when you were sixteen years old, not like I want to kiss you...."

He brought his lips to hers and savored the warmth and softness of her mouth. Her lips clung to his when he eased off the delicate pressure. Reeves could feel himself growing hard with arousal as he fought his drugging desire to kiss her again. And again. And again.

"Why couldn't you have kissed me like this that night of my birthday party?" She whispered the reprisal against his mouth.

"Because I was smarter back then. And a lot tougher."

Reeves couldn't help himself. He kissed her with the same lingering sweetness. She responded, her breathing becoming more shallow, like his. Then they were kissing harder, lips parted, only their mouths touching, the contact growing slippery and wet. Reeves felt her hands framing his face at the same moment that he slipped his hand around the back of her neck and plunged it up into her hair to cup her head.

"God, I want you," he muttered as he sent his tongue inside her mouth. But the words didn't make her bar the deeper intimacy.

Somehow he had to make *her* stop kissing *him*. It was his only hope of calling a halt. The lack of control seemed more than physical. Some other hunger besides sex was raging inside Reeves. Some unknown powerful satisfaction swelled his chest. The alarm going off in his head was one whose ringing he hadn't ever heard before. Until he understood its exact nature, he needed to *stop*.

Reeves felt for her zipper and started to slide it down her back. She gasped and stiffened and pulled away. He zipped up her dress before he sat upright in his seat, trying to compose himself.

"What the hell was that all about?" he asked, because he didn't dare allow himself anything other than an aggressive reaction.

She didn't rise to his bait. Her reply was short-winded and embarrassed, but dignified.

"You know very well what it was about. It was about a man and a woman who could easily go to bed together, but won't."

Reeves sucked in a long, audible breath. Against all his better judgment, he urged, "We could spend one night together. Go to a motel and finish what we started here."

"Let's finish what we started here by *not* going to a motel."

Her rejection of his proposition was as welcome as it was crushing. He knew damned well that he wouldn't be *finishing* anything by making love to her.

"You're probably right. Can I call you?" he asked, with the same ambivalence.

She shook her head emphatically. "No, don't call me. And I'm holding you to your word. Now please don't bother to get out. You can see me to my apartment door from here."

Reeves touched his hand to an imaginary chauffeur's hat. "Whatever you say, miss."

For a moment he thought she might slap his face. He almost wished that she would, partly because he deserved to be slapped.

"How can you be so disrespectful, mocking your own father!" she reprimanded him. "When you get back to your condo on St. Charles Avenue, take a good look in the mirror. You'll see a grown-up version of a little boy with a big chip on his shoulder."

She got out of the car and slammed the door. Reeves winced. Gripping the leather-covered wheel in both hands, he sat there, watching her march to the entrance of her town house apartment, head high. He admired, as he always had, her queenly carriage.

Her posture was probably genetic, he reflected, badly needing to feel cynical. Underneath the graciousness, she still had a princess complex. Her inbred snobbery was intact, whether she admitted it or not. Proof of that was her dumping those two poor bastards after she'd met their middle-class families.

Where did that leave him, the son of former servants?

If Olivia had any perception about people, she should understand that he'd needed that chip on his shoulder when he was growing up. He'd needed the toughness. Hell, he needed that chip now when he was feeling vulnerable and rejected.

What was the name of those two unlucky guys who had been engaged to her? Eric and somebody.

Starting up the Porsche to make the long drive from Metairie to uptown New Orleans, Reeves searched his memory.

Olivia held back her tears until she was inside her apartment. Slumped against the door, she wept without restraint.

She was just so *angry*. Tomorrow she would be fine. In a week or two she would have stopped thinking about tonight. A month from now she would have put Reeves Talbot out of her mind.

This date would fade in her memory. She would cope with the disappointment in him, survive the unpleasantness of the encounter with William. This awful misery would go away. Olivia had been miserable before— and disappointed and angry.

Life would go on.

Chapter Five

"That serve of yours was vicious today," Alan complained mildly. "In fact, you played like a man with a grudge against a tennis ball. These poor balls aren't even good for practice after that punishment." He tossed a clear plastic cylinder containing three chartreuse tennis balls into a nearby trash bin.

"I was trying to vent my frustrations," Reeves admitted.

The two men were headed toward the men's locker room on Saturday morning after playing singles at the Hilton River Center.

"Legal frustrations?"

"No, male frustrations. Woman problem," Reeves added tersely.

Two weeks had gone by since his date with Olivia, and he couldn't stop thinking about her. It was driving him nuts.

He wanted to see her again. The urge got stronger every day, instead of easing and going away. Reeves had been infatuated with women before, but never like this.

"Well, I hope you get some relief before I face you across the net again, Counselor," Alan said, slapping Reeves on the back.

"I'm going to try to deal with my problem today."

He was going to go back on his word and call her.

The sense of treading into dangerous waters if he got involved with her had faded. He could handle a relationship with her. After a few dates, probably the fascination would die a natural death. He might find that he didn't *like* her. She might prove to be vain and shallow under her facade of poise and dignity.

Reeves didn't waste any time calling. From the Hilton he drove straight to his condo on St. Charles. Entering, he dropped his tennis bag and went directly to the nearest phone, which was located in what was meant to be a dining room. Reeves used the room for a home office.

Like the rest of the place, it was inadequately furnished and poorly decorated, with lots of blank wall space. The man-size swivel chair upholstered in dark green leather and the massive oak desk had come from a secondhand furniture store on Magazine Street. Seated upright in the chair, Reeves punched out the digits of Olivia's telephone number from memory. Then he sprawled back, holding the receiver to his ear, and glanced at his Rolex. It was quarter to eleven. Would she be home?

On the second ring a female voice answered. Not her voice, but presumably that of her apartment mate. Reeves prepared himself for the disappointing news that Olivia was out.

"May I speak to Olivia, if she's there," he requested. "This is Reeves Talbot calling."

"I'm sorry, but Olivia isn't in. I'll tell her that you called."

Where was she? Had she gotten up and gone somewhere? Or had she spent the night with a man and not come home yet? Reeves had to know.

"I was hoping to catch her before she left."

"Oh, she's been gone for hours."

"Has she? On a Saturday morning?" Reeves conveyed a casual, interested surprise, hoping to elicit information about Olivia's whereabouts. He might be able to track her down if she had gone shopping.

"On Saturday mornings Olivia does volunteer social work."

A dry, humorous inflection told Reeves that the apartment mate was speaking tongue-in-cheek. "Social work?" he repeated.

"She plays chauffeur and maid for four old ladies, making it possible for them to have a bridge party with a fancy lunch."

"Every Saturday? Are they rich old ladies who might include her in their wills?" Reeves fished for a self-serving motive.

"No, if they were, I would alternate Saturday mornings with her and try to get written in myself," she wisecracked. "As it is, she twists my arm to pinch-hit for her if she gets sick or something momentous comes up. The old ladies are anything but thrilled since my idea of an elegant lunch is a chicken salad sandwich on a paper plate. By the way, I'm Judy Hays, Olivia's chatty apartment mate."

"It's nice to meet you over the phone, Judy."

"Would you like to leave a number, in case Olivia wants to return your call?"

"Thank you, I would." He gave her two numbers—his home number and his office number. "Would you also give her the message that if I don't hear from her, I'll keep calling."

"In other words, she might as well return your call."

"Something like that." Reeves's grin of appreciation for her lack of subtlety was in his voice.

"It's not an easy matter catching her in. She's a busy woman, what with planning social functions for people free of charge."

"Oh?"

"Olivia's our resident Miss Manners out here in Metairie."

"I see."

"If I could convince her to go into the social consulting business and let me be her manager, we could both resign from our jobs. But no luck." She sighed an exaggerated sigh. "You'd think that making money was in bad taste."

Volunteer work was a part of Olivia's background. Reeves understood that perfectly, even if her aprtment mate didn't.

Olivia's charitable instinct, however admirable, carried overtones of snobbery for him. Hers was a distinctive *type* of charitable instinct, a high-class kind of helpfulness to society.

It wasn't baking cookies for the PTA or organizing a garage sale to raise money for the Girl Scouts—lower-class charitable projects she might have been expected to undertake if she'd married Eric or Sam.

"Well, it was nice talking to you, Reeves. I'm going out shopping, but I'll leave a note for Olivia."

Don't bother, I'll call back later. Those were the words he should have said, giving himself an out.

Instead, he thanked her and said, ''Please do that.''

Olivia read Judy's message, written in her lefty's slanted script and stuck to the inside of the apartment door. The note ended with *If you don't want him, maybe you could give him to me for my birthday. I love his deep voice.*

She sighed and made the troubling admission, ''So do I, Judy.''

Holding the note with the two telephone numbers, Olivia walked slowly into the living room and perched on the edge of the sofa, within reach of the phone located on an end table. She glanced at her watch, as though the time had some bearing on whether she would pick up the receiver and call Reeves. It was one-forty-five in the afternoon.

If she called him at his home number, the phone would ring somewhere in her old home.

She would keep that thought in mind and go ahead and return his call, Olivia decided. As likely as not, she would get his answering machine and wouldn't have to talk to him.

Punching out the digits and then putting the receiver to her ear, she mentally rehearsed a dignified message. *This is Olivia Prescott. Please honor your promise, Reeves, and don't call me again. Thank you.*

He answered on the first ring, a note of expectation in his voice. ''Hello.''

''You must have been sitting on top of the phone.'' In her surprise, Olivia sounded flustered, not in the least dignified. ''I was expecting an answering machine. This is Olivia Prescott," she added, as though he might not have recognized her voice.

"I'm stationed near the phone, trying to write a brief and keeping a vigil in the event that you did return my call. How have you been?" he inquired conversationally.

"I've been just fine."

"Lucky you. I haven't been doing so good. My concentration has been shot to hell lately. I haven't been sleeping very soundly. And I've lost my appetite. All classic symptoms of lovesickness, of course," he declared.

"I'm sure that's an ailment you've contracted lots of times before," Olivia said. She was thrown off balance by his coming on with such a ridiculous line. And she wasn't any more immune to the pleasure of hearing his voice than Judy was.

"I've never had quite this severe a case. What I've done in the past is let the illness run its course in a relationship, not try to cure it. Eventually I recovered."

"You have a real problem this time then, don't you? You'll have to discover another remedy."

"I feel better just talking to you and hearing your voice. Do you have a few minutes to talk?"

"You promised that you wouldn't call, Reeves."

"I managed not to call for two weeks. What would be the harm in talking to me on the phone?" he cajoled. "Tell me about this Saturday morning bridge party Judy mentioned. Who are the four elderly ladies. Friends of your grandmother's?"

"Judy is so indiscreet!" Olivia exclaimed, exasperated. "She probably filled you in on every detail of my life!"

"I pulled the information out of her. Blame me."

"I should hang up on you."

"That would be rude," he chided. "Please don't hang up."

Olivia sat back on the sofa with a loud sigh meant for his ears. The whole trouble was that she didn't want to hang up. She wanted to stay on the line and talk to him. "At least spare me the corny line."

"It's not altogether a line," he said ruefully. "So what's the story on the four old ladies? Who are they?"

"Two of them are sisters, both widowed. They had homes in Old Metairie at one time. Now they live together in a condominium there. I met them when I was dating their nephew."

"Not Eric or Sam?"

"No. What a memory you have!" Olivia marveled.

"Go on," he said. "I didn't mean to interrupt."

"After I broke up with him, I still visited them occasionally and had tea with them. It seemed to mean so much to them, and I thought they were sweet. They were starved not just for company, but for an excuse to bring out their best china teacups. The bridge game evolved. I learned that they had belonged to bridge clubs for most of their adult lives. The other two old ladies are longtime acquaintances and bridge players, too. One lives in a nursing home and one lives with a daughter who works. That's the story in a nutshell."

"And how long have you been doing this?"

"About a year and a half, I guess."

"For a year and a half, you've given up your Saturday mornings for four elderly people who are no relation? Are you working on sainthood?" he inquired, sounding oddly reproachful. "Is there some human motive a cynic like me can understand? You aren't carrying a torch for the nephew, are you?"

"No, definitely not. And giving up my Saturday mornings isn't a sacrifice. I feel the same way I would feel if I were doing something nice for four great-aunts. They're very sweet and appreciative. Now does that satisfy your curiosity?"

"On that one topic, more or less. Do you like going to movies? We didn't touch on that subject at all on our date."

"Reeves, I'm not going to stay on the phone with you all afternoon discussing random topics," Olivia protested.

"Actually, the subject of movies isn't a random topic," he replied. "My next question was going to be, 'Have you seen Kevin Costner's latest movie?' If you hadn't, I was going to ask whether you'd like to take in a matinee. Have you seen it?"

"No."

"Would you like to take in a matinee? I figure you probably have plans for tonight."

"I do."

"How about it? I'll pick you up in twenty minutes. I'll be wearing jeans and running shoes. A shirt, too, naturally. In the meanwhile you can check the movie listings in the newspaper and find out which theater is showing the Costner film."

"Reeves—"

"Or pick out another movie if you don't like Kevin Costner."

"I *like* Kevin Costner as an actor. The choice of a movie isn't the issue. It's whether I think that I should go out on another date with you."

"It's not really a date."

"It *is* a date. I thought we were in complete agreement that we shouldn't see each other. Shouldn't get involved."

"How involved can two people get sitting in a crowd of moviegoers and crunching kernels of popcorn? Please. See the movie with me," he urged. "It's bright daylight outside. What's the harm?"

Olivia couldn't hold out against herself and him, too. "Okay." she gave in weakly. "I do want to see that movie. But we'll go in my car, not yours." As though less exciting transportation would cancel out the element of compromise.

"Whatever you say. You can pay for the tickets and popcorn, for all I care," he said cheerfully. "See you in twenty minutes, with or without a speeding ticket. Do me a favor and try to look your least beautiful. Wipe out the vision of loveliness that I've been living with the last two weeks."

"I won't even check my teeth for remnants of the spinach salad I had for lunch," she promised him.

Hanging up, Olivia was smiling despite her troubling conviction. *This is a mistake. I should have turned him down.*

She felt ridiculously young as she raced upstairs to her bedroom and changed clothes, shedding a pretty skirt-and-blouse outfit in a violet print and donning khaki slacks and a plain white blouse. After a brief struggle with herself not to thrust her feet into red sandals and wear a matching red belt, she stepped into straw-colored espadrilles.

Resisting the temptation to add a scarf or accent jewelry, she contented herself with applying red lip gloss and went back downstairs. It added to the fun somehow that in the spirit of cooperation Olivia was going against all her instincts for dressing with a flair.

He rang the doorbell twice in quick succession, then a third time as though for good measure. Evidently he was in a carefree mood, too. Slinging the strap of her tiny shoulder bag over one shoulder, she half ran to the door.

In his casual attire, he was all fit, rugged man from windblown dark brown hair to athletic shoes. His short-sleeved cotton knit shirt, open at the neck, exposed a strong column of throat and hugged his well-developed chest. The shirt was tucked into the waistband of his jeans. From there down, were no disappointments to her woman's eye.

Stepping out, keys in hand, Olivia presented herself for his inspection. "Just call me Plain Jane," she said. "You asked for the daytime me. You have it."

Reeves reached with one hand and lightly held her chin. He tilted it upward, scrutinizing her face in the bright sunlight. Olivia squinted against the glare.

"Not a blemish in that beautiful complexion," he complained.

She wiggled her nose and made a face at him. "Beauty is only skin-deep. Handsome is as handsome does."

Before he dropped his hand, he gave her chin a gentle squeeze. For a breathless instant, Olivia thought he might bend and drop a kiss on her lips.

She locked the door and led the way to her conservative compact car that was several years old. His racy white Porsche was parked in a visitors' parking spot. She waited for him to make some offer that they might take it instead, but he didn't. Unlocking the driver's door while he strode around to the passenger's side, Olivia couldn't resist poking a little good-natured fun at him.

"Don't tell me that I've finally run across a man who isn't macho," she mused. "Most men have this lordly sense of superiority when it comes to deciding who's going to drive, him or me, and whether we're riding in his car or mine."

He grinned at her across the roof of the car. "I'm willing to risk my neck and ride a short distance in this engineering marvel of yours."

"Then get in and fasten your seat belt," was her spirited response. "Or we can take your car, and I'll drive," she added. "I'm willing to compromise."

His grin faded, while hers spread her lips with devilish glee, giving away the fact that she'd been pulling his leg.

"Before I agree to that, you would have to take a little test drive in your car," he retorted.

"I wish you could have seen your face!" Olivia said, laughing. "You would think that I had suggested driving your precious Porsche into Lake Pontchartrain!"

"One point for you." He laughed along with her as he got in and made room for his long frame, pushing the seat back as far as it went. "Since when do you like to put people on?" he asked. "I never saw that side of your personality."

"You never gave me a chance to show many facets of my personality," Olivia pointed out without rancor. She started up the car. "I wasn't a humorless child. But growing up as I did without young parents and with no siblings, I didn't learn to tease and play practical jokes at home. You should hear my apartment mate, Judy, tell about growing up in her family."

"She has a country twang in her speech."

"She's from Ponchatoula. Her father is a strawberry farmer."

"Have you gone with her on visits?" he asked curiously.

"On a number of occasions. Her mom is a perfectly marvelous cook."

The conversation was easy and relaxed on the short drive to the theater. Olivia took the most direct route via Veterans Highway, its multiple lanes in either direction congested with traffic as always. On either side of the main commercial thoroughfare, buildings of every color and description and size were jumbled together mile after mile with no discernible urban plan, housing a great variety of business establishments that included numerous automobile dealerships, restaurants, furniture stores, strip shopping malls. Located some distance apart were Lakeside and Clearview shopping centers.

As familiar as she was with Veterans Highway, Olivia was always struck by its ugliness, a fact she commented on cheerfully.

"There's nothing picturesque about this whole stretch," Reeves agreed. "It's a prime example of urban blight." His condemnation was equable.

Their pleasure in each other was too great to allow drab surroundings to matter. It was as ordinary a date in every way as their date two weeks ago had been glamorous.

Olivia parked between two nondescript automobiles at the movie theater. She and Reeves walked to the ticket window, where there was a short line. He paid for the tickets. Inside he bought a large bucket of popcorn for them to share and a soft drink for each of them. Olivia carried the drinks, and he carried the popcorn.

They had to stand a few minutes outside the door of the theater showing their movie. Reeves sampled the popcorn and fed Olivia plump kernels. Popcorn had never tasted more delicious.

"Hmm. Good," she declared. "I've never understood why popcorn at movies is better than popcorn anywhere else."

"There must be some secret ingredient."

It was delightfully ordinary conversation. When Reeves flicked a particle from her lips, he was performing a wonderfully ordinary act. The light brush of his finger was proprietorial in the tradition of the casually attentive male escort.

A stream of moviegoers burst through the door, signaling that the earlier show had ended. Olivia and Reeves waited until the coast was clear and went inside, along with the small crowd that had collected. They sat in the middle of a center row of seats not too near the front.

"Perfect spot," Reeves said in a complacent tone, balancing the bucket of popcorn on his thigh.

Olivia was in complete agreement. They munched popcorn, waiting for the lights to dim and the movie to begin. Delving her hand into the bucket, she occasionally encountered his hand. With each contact a comfortable intimacy grew.

The movie was engrossing with tense, dramatic scenes. Oddly enough, Olivia's awareness of Reeves added to her involvement in the story line rather than interfering with it. She could sense that he was absorbed in the larger-than-life action on the screen, too.

When the popcorn bucket was empty, he set it on the floor and put his arm around the back of her chair. Olivia smiled at him in the semidarkness. He smiled back. Then they both turned their attention back to the movie.

After it had ended, they sat through the credits before getting up to leave. Olivia had always disliked jumping up and rushing out as soon as a movie was over, and Reeves was of the same mind, she now learned. In the aisle he took her hand, and they held hands until they'd reached her car in the parking lot.

"Let's go to Lakeside and walk through the mall," he said.

"Okay."

They had an hour and a half before she needed to go back to her apartment and get ready for her engagement that evening.

Reeves was silent on the way to Lakeside Shopping Center. Olivia glanced over at him and saw that his expression was sober and thoughtful.

"Am I making you nervous with my driving?" she asked lightly. "You haven't said a word since we got in the car."

"Haven't I? Well, your driving isn't the cause." He reached over and gave her nearest hand on the steering wheel a warm squeeze. "You can drive my Porsche anytime."

"Then I passed the competency test?"

"With flying colors. For a woman, you're a darned good driver."

"For a man, you're a good passenger."

The repartee was forced. They were both trying too hard. A new seriousness had entered in, spoiling the fun. The question "Where do we go from here?" was going to have to be answered.

Olivia was certain that Reeves had been grappling with it just now.

"When I woke up this morning, I certainly never dreamed that my day would include taking a walk in a shopping mall with you," she remarked as she found an empty spot in the vast parking lot at Lakeside.

"Same here," Reeves said.

"I could have invited you to my apartment, but Judy is probably there. Of course, she's dying to meet you anyway."

"I want to meet her, too, but another time."

This afternoon he preferred to be alone with her, even in the midst of strangers in a public place.

"There are other places where we could have gone for a walk," Olivia pointed out as they got out of the car. "West End, the lakefront."

Reeves took her hand and laced his fingers with hers. "We don't have much time. Why use half of it riding in a car? That was my logic."

"True."

They walked toward the nearest entrance.

"And the less scenic the setting, the better," he went on. "What place could be more ideal for getting a handle on reality than a shopping center?"

"A Schwegmann's Supermarket perhaps." The chain of giant supermarkets, a household name in New Orleans, sold everything from tires to jewelry in addition to grocery items. "But then we'd draw a lot of attention just browsing, not filling up a shopping cart. A store detective would probably be alerted to keep an eye on us."

Reeves smiled, apparently entertained by the image she'd evoked. "We could push a cart around, put a few items in it." His gaze locked with hers, and the amusement on his face faded. He shook his head. "Shopping in a damned Schwegmann's store with you appeals to me, Olivia."

She nodded. "It's the novelty. That would soon wear off."

"I have my doubts about 'soon.'"

They reached the double glass doors and entered the mall. The air-conditioned atmosphere was degrees cooler than the balmy spring air outside. Live plants growing in huge planters looked artificial. The polished tile floor had a hard, bright sheen.

Reeves tightened his grip on her hand as he guided her among the currents and eddies of humanity with shopping bags and parcels. After he and Olivia both had been bumped into several times, they headed as though by mutual consent toward an unoccupied bench out of the main traffic.

"Do you shop here?" he asked.

"Oh, yes. Also at Clearview. And Esplanade," she added.

"If it weren't so far out of the way, we should have gone there. I've never seen it."

"It's a pretty shopping center with two levels. The big Macy's is the main draw. With a Macy's and a Lord & Taylor's and a Saks in downtown New Orleans, there's no need for you to travel to the suburbs to spend your money."

Reeves drew in a sharp breath. His mind obviously wasn't on the conversation any more than Olivia's was.

"I'll move somewhere else," he said. "Preferably another uptown location, if that's not objectionable. Or I could live in the French Quarter."

"Move?" she blurted out, as dismayed as she was astonished. "You can't *move* because—because of *me*. That's ridiculous. What would you do with your condominium?"

"Put it on the market. Lease it." He shrugged.

"Don't be absurd. You can't make that kind of major accommodation out of consideration for my feelings. I won't let you."

"I don't see any alternative. Even if you got an apartment by yourself, I still don't want the place where I live to be off-limits to you."

"Reeves, we might see each other for a few weeks and go our separate ways again. By the time you were settling in a new location, our attraction might already be burned out. No." She shook her head, adamant.

"If that turns out to be the situation, so be it. I won't blame you. I want those few weeks enough to go to almost any lengths, Olivia." His voice was fervent and sure.

A shiver ran along Olivia's spine. She felt a knot of dread in her stomach at what she was thinking.

"There's no reason that you should have to move. I could visit you there."

"You know it would be too painful," Reeves protested gruffly. "I couldn't ask you to do that."

"A psychiatrist would probably consider it good therapy."

"I don't want spending time with me to be therapy," he objected.

"You bought your condominium because apparently it suited your needs," she insisted.

He searched her face. "Is the problem that you don't really want to give us a chance? Would you rather my living at your old address be a sensitive issue between us?"

Olivia pulled her hand free of his.

"Moving wouldn't change the fact that you wanted to own a piece of the Prescott mansion, Reeves."

"We're back to the chip on my shoulder, aren't we?" He sighed. "Okay. I give in. We'll try having you visit me and see how it goes. I'll agree to almost anything as long as I can see you."

He leaned over and kissed her on the lips. Olivia closed her eyes at the warm contact, and her breath caught in her throat over the sheer delight of his nearness. Her hand came up to touch his face.

"Spend tomorrow with me?" he urged, pulling back a few inches to look into her eyes. "The whole day. I'll pick you up in the morning. We could have a champagne brunch in the Quarter and make up plans as we go along."

"No..."

He kissed her again. "Or we could head across the causeway. I hear there are some great little restaurants in Madisonville on the riverfront. Please say yes."

"Yes, I'll spend the day with you, but don't pick me up. That's what I was going to say." Olivia paused, courage failing her. She *couldn't*. Yes, she *could*. "I'll drive myself and come to your place on St. Charles. We can go together from there."

Chapter Six

Why was she subjecting herself to the pain and sadness of visiting Reeves in her former home?

Olivia's sense of necessity was complex. Some of it had to do with distrust. Before she spent any more time in Reeves's company or got drawn any deeper into a relationship with him, she needed to confront the grownup man on St. Charles Avenue in the setting where she'd known him as a boy and a young man. She didn't trust her own feelings toward him or his feelings toward her.

Was he attracted to *her,* the person she was now? Or was he pursuing some creation in his own mind? Was she attracted to *him,* the thirty-four-year-old successful plaintiff attorney, or was she caught up in his romantic scenario and making an old conquest?

Before things went any further, Olivia needed answers to those questions.

Too, she felt a morbid curiosity to see for herself the alterations to the mansion that the developers had made. Then maybe she would reach a state of acceptance and not recoil at the very idea of her old home being redone as condominiums.

After all, the developers had saved it from falling into a bad state of deterioration and having to be torn down. How much worse it would be to drive by and see some new building erected on the same site.

Mixed in with Olivia's dread was a longing to return to her old home, however changed it was on the interior.

The Prescott mansion had been built at the turn of the century by Randolph Prescott, her grandfather's uncle, after whom he had been named. It was constructed of pale gray granite in the architectural style of a French château, minus turrets and fake embellishments. For all its somber, imposing aspect, it combined grace and elegance.

Olivia could count on one hand the number of times that she had driven past the mansion during the past eight years. She'd avoided St. Charles Avenue, once her personal dominion. When she'd lived there, she hadn't noticed how many large, branching live-oak trees shaded the avenue. She hadn't consciously appreciated the historic uniqueness. Old-fashioned streetcars rumbling along on their tracks on the broad grassy median, called the "neutral ground" in New Orleans, had been a daily, familiar sight, as much taken for granted as the sun rising and setting.

She hadn't ridden the streetcars. They provided transportation for ordinary people, not rich people living in a mansion with a chauffeur.

Reeves probably had ridden the streetcars, Olivia reflected, stopping at a light several blocks away from her destination. He must have traveled around the city on public buses, too. They'd grown up in the same location and yet lived totally different existences. Now he was having a turn at living in the mansion.

Lately she had grown more used to the idea. Much of her original shock and outrage had faded, but she was still bothered by his having chosen to live there, of all places.

The light turned green and Olivia proceeded, her nerves tightening. Driving the last block, she gripped the wheel tight to keep from making a U-turn. *You can always go on past,* she promised herself, her eyes picking out familiar landmarks and passing over the unfamiliar. There was a heartbreaking sense of going home.

Let everything be very strange and different, she prayed, realizing that change would be easier than familiarity.

Reeves had given advance warning that while the front lawn and landscaping had been retained for show, much of the rear gardens had been eliminated out of practical necessity. A great majority of the extensive area between the mansion and the carriage house was now paved with flagstones. Secure garaged parking had been provided for the condominium owners. The entrance was from a side street. It once had been the service entrance.

Olivia parked her car in a visitor's spot. Before she could get out, Reeves was there to open her door. He apparently had come out to wait for her.

Instead of helping her get out of the car, he leaned down to talk to her, blocking her way.

"Hi," he greeted. "I thought you might call and make different arrangements."

"No. Here I am." Olivia was touched by the concern and sympathy in his voice and in his face.

"You look pretty," he complimented with the same gentle note. "I like that pink color on you."

She was wearing a pale pink linen skirt with a pink-and-white, candy-striped blouse.

"Thank you." Olivia picked up her white purse from the passenger's seat, but he still didn't step back. Being trapped wasn't unpleasant. His clean masculine scent filled her lungs. He looked handsome and clean-cut in tan slacks, a blue shirt open at the neck and a navy blazer.

"Are you sure you want to go through with this?" he asked. "Our reservation for brunch isn't until eleven, but we could have coffee in the French Quarter, walk around and work up an appetite." Instead of going inside and having coffee in his condominium.

"Now that I'm here, I want to go inside."

He sighed. "All right. But I warn you. I haven't done much in the way of furnishing and decorating my condo. Well, you'll see." He finally stepped back.

Olivia got out and stood next to him, glancing around. Reeves followed her gaze as it came to rest on the carriage house, built of the same dove-gray granite as the mansion itself. She knew from a newspaper article published several years ago that the carriage house was a condominium unit, too. Why hadn't he chosen to be the owner of that condominium unit instead of one of the units in the mansion?

Reeves seemed to read the question in her mind. "The carriage house was snapped up by a friend of the devel-

opers before they'd even begun the renovation," he remarked. It hadn't been available for him to buy.

"Why was it snapped up? Was it less expensive?"

He shook his head. "No. Actually it was more expensive, since it's larger than the others, with three bedrooms rather than two. Plus, it's more private, set off to
itself."

She voiced the obvious irony aloud. "So the servants' quarters turns out to be the most desirable place
to live. There has to be some democratic justice in that."

"The servants' quarters wasn't a bad place to live
when I was growing up."

Olivia smiled a forced, wan smile. "Neither was the
mansion. Shall we go inside?"

"Sure."

Her earlier prayer was answered. She might have been
entering a strange apartment building. The decor was
elegant and impersonal. Reeves took her a short distance down a marble-tiled hallway to his door, which
bore a brass number. From the general location of his
condominium on the first floor, she surmised that the
original rooms had perhaps included the kitchen where
his mother had cooked meals. Had that been a factor in
his buying this particular condominium?

Again he seemed to follow her thoughts. He answered her unasked question as he unlocked the door.

"This was the only unit for sale in the building at the
time that I was looking for a condo. The owner was
anxious to get out from under his mortgage. He jumped
at my first offer, which was quite a bit lower than his
asking price."

Reeves pushed open the door and gestured for her to
enter. Olivia stepped into an empty foyer with blank
walls painted a soft peach shade.

"I feel like Alice stepping through the looking glass," she said, her throat suddenly tight. "This is so bizarre. I wonder if they kept any of the original rooms intact." Upstairs, her old bedroom and playroom were a part of some stranger's condo.

"I assume that they must have." His voice was gruff with understanding. "I'm not very well acquainted with my neighbors. The only other condo I've gotten a look at is the one next to mine. Have you seen enough?" he inquired.

Olivia shook her head. "I'll be okay. Give me a guided tour."

"The kindest thing you can say is that I haven't decorated the place in poor taste. I had the same furniture in a cramped one-bedroom apartment."

"Judging from the size of this foyer, your rooms are nice and spacious." Finding his hint of insecurity appealing, Olivia took the lead, walking from room to room with him following close behind her.

He hadn't been exaggerating when he said that he hadn't done much with furnishing and decoration. There were blank walls throughout, and furniture was sparse. In the bright, modern kitchen, he had two stools at a breakfast bar, the only seating for dining. Living room furniture consisted of a long black leather sofa, an Eames chair, also black leather, a cocktail table and a floor lamp.

He'd adapted the dining room for use as a rudimentary office with a man-size oak desk, a swivel chair, a freestanding bookcase and a filing cabinet. The smaller of the two bedrooms contained cardboard boxes with books and odds and ends. The master bedroom had a low king-size bed with a walnut headboard and a matching bureau. A floor lamp was placed to function as a reading light.

"There's plenty of closet space."

He opened the door to a walk-in closet. Obligingly Olivia walked over and peered in.

"You certainly are neat. Or did you straighten up for me?"

He grinned sheepishly. "I was up at dawn vacuuming and dusting."

The master bathroom had a whirlpool tub as well as a separate shower enclosure. His toilet articles were lined up on the marble vanity, which had two sinks. The tang of his after-shave scented the air, and a damp towel hung on the brass towel bar.

"Very luxurious," Olivia commented approvingly. "I could envy you this bathroom. I could envy you the entire condo," she added.

"If it were somewhere else."

"Anywhere else."

Sad awareness engulfed her, and she struggled to contain sudden poignant emotion.

"Maybe we could go now—" Her voice, husky with the tears clogging her throat, broke in the middle of her request.

Reeves opened his arms, offering comfort, and she went into them. He hugged her tightly.

"I'm sorry, sweetheart," he murmured. "I was afraid this would be too hard on you."

Olivia burrowed her cheek against his chest. "My grandmother had her stroke here. She died in her bed."

"I know. I know."

"My grandfather took his life here two weeks after her funeral. He shot himself in his study."

"I know all that. Don't torture yourself thinking about it. I could kick myself for letting you come." Reeves's voice was fierce with tenderness. "I'll sell the damned condo."

"No. No, you can't do that because of me." She twisted her head violently in objection.

"The hell I can't." His fingers thrust gently into her hair, and he held her head still against him. "Try not to feel sad, sweetheart. In just a minute when you're up to it, we'll go."

Olivia's tears had dried up without spilling over. Somehow his strength and caring response had soothed her anguish so that it wasn't necessary to shed tears. She wanted to stay right there in his arms, safe and protected. The urge to *depend* on him and trust herself to him was alarmingly powerful.

"I'm okay," she said, mustering resistance. "But I'll bet your shirt is a mess. I'll bet I got lipstick on it."

"So what if you did? I have other shirts."

He loosened his arms, but didn't release her as she raised her head. They both examined the damage. Smears of pink lipstick decorated his shirtfront in the vee of his jacket lapels.

"I must not have any lipstick left on my lips," Olivia conjectured with a little grimace of apology.

"Not much," Reeves confirmed in a husky tone, gazing at her mouth. He bent his head and pressed his mouth to hers, as though blotting up the minor residue. For all his gentleness, the kiss contained hunger and passion held in check.

Passion seemed a safe emotional outlet, much safer than tenderness and caring. Olivia slipped her arms around his neck. He ended the kiss, pulling back and gazing down at her with the same suppressed desire.

"I'll have the shirt cleaned for you," she promised softly, and there was other promise in her voice.

"Don't be silly. Why don't you wait for me in the living room?" he suggested. "I won't be five minutes." His arms tightened a fraction rather than falling away, his body obviously at war with his words.

"I'll use your powder room and repair my makeup."

"You can use my bathroom."

The permission bestowed intimate privileges. Olivia felt a warm flush of sexual languor seeping through her, a subtle involuntary seductiveness. It was such an appealing idea to be in the next room while he was taking off his shirt, stripping to his waist and baring his broad shoulders and muscular chest.

"Or maybe you shouldn't use my bathroom," Reeves said. "I'm only human. My honorable instincts might lose out."

"I would be surprised if they did," Olivia replied, smiling at him. "You're a very nice man, Reeves. A lot more sensitive than I would ever have expected."

She drew his head down and kissed him on the mouth, a sweet kiss of gratitude. He groaned and gathered her close in a crushing embrace that let her feel his strength. Olivia absorbed into her pores his rugged masculinity, his toughness, which had always attracted her to him.

"Olivia, I *want* you. So much that I would take advantage of you when your defenses are down. Don't *let* me." His words were a rough plea, but one hand stroked down her back and along her hip with a lover's intention.

"My defenses aren't down, Reeves. I'm a grown woman who can look after herself."

She stroked the breadth of his shoulders, not with deliberate provocation, but for her own pleasure. A little shudder ran through his big body, and all his resistance was gone. Passion took over.

"I want you," he said again, and the words were a part of lovemaking, not a warning or a plea for control.

They kissed, his hunger unleashed, his insatiable need awakening her own woman's needs.

Olivia responded with delight to his caresses as he explored her body, first while she was fully clothed. She moaned when he cupped her breasts through her blouse, squeezed gently, rubbed her hard nipples with his palms. Her own hands were busy, stroking his chest, slipping around under his jacket to his back.

She wanted to luxuriate in touching him, and yet the pleasure of his touch was too excruciating and wonderful. *Go slowly, very slowly* battled with *Hurry, oh, please, hurry.* The latter impulse gaining ground, Olivia's hand followed an intimate path downward. He went still and taut with suspense and then lax, totally at her tender mercy, as delicately she fondled him, finding him hard and swollen and ready to make love to her.

He stopped her, his hand stilling hers and pressing it into harder contact. "Do you want me, Olivia, even a particle as much as I want you?" he demanded, searching her face.

The seriousness in his voice and expression made the question disturbing. He seemed to be asking more than *Was she as sexually aroused as he was?* Some of the alarm she'd felt earlier was revived. At this point, all that she was willing to risk in a relationship was physical intimacy and friendship.

"If we took off our clothes, you could discover the answer for yourself," she replied.

For a moment he looked into her eyes, doubtful and disappointed. Olivia gazed back, holding on to her inability to trust him.

"I think I know the answer, but I still want to take you to bed," he said, and kissed her, ending the discussion.

They began shedding their clothes. He was faster and more efficient than she was. When he was completely naked, brawny and fit and fully aroused, Olivia was just tossing aside her panty hose and was only bare to the waist. She let him take over undressing her, a procedure that turned into delicious torture.

While he unzipped and lowered her skirt, he was bending over and kissing her breasts. She arched her back and swelled her chest for him, murmuring aloud her pleasure as he nuzzled and licked and tasted, then bit gently with his teeth.

Dropping to his knees in front of her, he helped her step out of the skirt. Her only remaining garment now was her lacy bikini panties. He seemed in no hurry to remove them, first caressing her stomach with his palm and next her hips and buttocks. Finally he hooked his fingers under the elastic and revealed her slowly, inch by inch.

Olivia was weak with the erotic suspense by the time he was able to stop and comb through her luxuriant triangle of black curls. Her knees buckled as he slipped his hand between her thighs and pronounced in a low, deeply pleased male tone, "I might drown if I kissed you down here."

He immediately hazarded his chances. She whispered his name helplessly, opening to the warm, rough invasion of his tongue, which penetrated to the heart of her desire. Piercing pleasure burned away any figment of modesty and freed her to the ultimate in sensual enjoyment.

"Please," she begged, and he rose and picked her up in his arms. Reaching the bed, he laid her down as though she were delicate and precious. Olivia could feel a tremor in his muscles.

The mechanics of making love seemed to take on a disturbing meaningfulness as she helped him with the condom and then as he placed himself in position, his big frame levered over hers. It was more than sexually stimulating when Reeves gazed at the juncture of their bodies, not yet complete. He penetrated slowly, seeming to take forever and going incredibly deep.

Olivia opened her mouth to say something, anything, to kill the emotional significance. Before she could get a word out, he cut off speech, sealing her lips with his as he pushed even deeper and began a devastatingly slow rhythm.

He filled her, satisfied some core need even as he built up intense desire for more and still more pleasure. Olivia sheathed him tightly, cushioned his thrusts. Theirs was a perfect physical union, unendurably wonderful. *It's only because this is the first time with him,* Olivia told herself on a wild surge toward ecstasy.

"I'm almost there, sweetheart," he warned with pained jubilation in his voice. "Come with me. *Now—*"

She tried to hold back and not reach climax at the exact moment he did, but the jolt of his body triggered her release. Stripped of all emotional protection, she was merged with him, flesh of his flesh, spirit of his spirit.

He lay slumped on top of her for mere seconds, then gathered her limp weight in his arms and took her with him as he rolled onto his side. Olivia lay there, her legs tangled with his, drowning in contentment.

"In case you're wondering, that was good for me," she mumbled, obeying the instinct for self-preservation that said, *Say something.*

His only answer was a shuddering intake of breath and a convulsive squeeze.

"You're a fantastic lover," she praised, his muteness making conversation that much more necessary. Again, he didn't answer. "Don't you talk after making love?"

Reeves gave her another bone-crushing squeeze. She could feel the vibration in his deep chest as he finally spoke.

"I don't think either one of us wants to hear what I might say right now."

The gravity in his tone put Olivia in a panic even while it flooded her with a sweet excitement. "Don't say it then. I'll let you lie here in peace and recover while I go to the bathroom and make myself presentable."

He raised up on his elbow and looked down at her. Olivia was as alarmed as she was thrilled by the tenderness and ardor in his face.

"And what if I don't recover in that amount of time?" he asked.

"Hunger pangs will probably bring you back to normal," she predicted. "It could easily take me a half hour to dress and repair the damage."

"There isn't any damage. You look beautiful." He brushed a strand of hair aside and bent to kiss her on the forehead.

"Sex affects your eyesight." Meaning to give him a friendly pat on the cheek, Olivia raised her hand and ended up caressing his face instead.

He closed his eyes, sucked in a deep breath and sat up, after carefully withdrawing.

"If you could cut that half hour to fifteen minutes, we can make our brunch reservation," he reflected, consulting his watch. "A Bloody Mary would really hit the spot right now." He climbed out of bed.

Olivia sat up, struggling to overcome her sense of rejection. He'd recovered very fast for someone who'd voiced doubts about ever recovering from the aftermath of making love. So much for his sincerity.

"A Bloody Mary would taste good," she agreed. "But then so would a champagne cocktail with orange juice."

"Whatever your heart desires," he declared, going over to pick up his clothes.

They took turns in the bathroom and got dressed again. Reeves was casually affectionate. Olivia was tempted to believe that she must have imagined his earlier seriousness.

Meeting in the center of his bedroom, ready to go, they inspected each other appreciatively.

"You look very handsome," Olivia complimented.

"You look even lovelier than you did when you arrived. Your complexion has a glow that it didn't have before. I wonder why," he mused.

"Probably for the same reason that you're wearing that smug, self-satisfied expression," she retorted. "Try to appear a little less proud of yourself, if you can. We don't want to advertise to the world what we've been up to."

"I'll try, for your sake. Personally, I really don't give a damn if the world knows."

He offered her his arm. Olivia took it, aware that the glow he'd mentioned was visible evidence of a happy state of mind.

They were almost out the door when the several phones in the condominium came to life. Reeves halted, glancing back.

"My answering machine will take it," he said. "Let's just wait a minute and make sure there's no emergency."

After a short interim, a woman's voice could be heard clearly, coming from his office. *"Mr. Talbot, this is Rachel Wade. I hate to bother you on a Sunday, but I'm about at my wit's end. My husband, Bill, is in terrible low spirits—"*

"I'd better talk to her," Reeves said. "Excuse me, will you?"

He bolted toward the office. Olivia stepped back inside to wait for him. The female voice, uneducated and worried, was continuing.

"—hate to ask you to advance us more money until you win our lawsuit against Bill's doctor. But the pharmacist won't fill Bill's prescriptions if we don't pay—"

"Mrs. Wade, Reeves Talbot here. Could you hold a moment?"

Reeves had picked up the phone. Before he carried on his conversation with his caller, he closed the door so that Olivia couldn't hear.

She realized that his great rush to get to the phone had been to cut off the message before the woman, the wife of a client suing his doctor, could reveal more details. Reeves evidently didn't trust Olivia to keep confidential any information she inadvertently learned about one of his cases. The knowledge offended her.

The phone call came as a distasteful reminder of the type of legal work that he did, filing lawsuits. Apparently, Reeves lent his clients money, gambling that he would win their cases and be paid back out of the sum awarded. That sort of policy might not be illegal or unethical, but it seemed questionable to her.

So many plaintiff attorneys made a bad impression on the public. They advertised for injury patients. They wore flashy, cheap clothes. They banded together to form their own shyster firms because no dignified, reputable firm would have them.

Olivia was greatly bothered that Reeves might be grouped in the same fraternity. She reminded herself that he would soon be joining Duplantis & Duplantis.

Chapter Seven

Reeves was fervently thankful that Rachel Wade hadn't mentioned Bella's name in her message. What disastrous timing that would have been. Sooner or later, Olivia would have to find out that he had taken a malpractice case against Dr. Bella, but he didn't plan on her finding out today.

He selfishly wished that he'd missed the phone call. It was an intrusion of reality, and he didn't want to deal with reality today.

For the first time ever when he was making love, he'd had to choke back the words, *I love you.* Then afterward he'd wanted to say them. Getting dressed with her, he'd still wanted to say them. He hadn't because he knew she wouldn't want to hear those words from him. Blurting out that he loved her would stop their affair before it got started.

And what he felt might not *be* love. It might be some stronger infatuation than he'd ever felt before. All he knew was that his feelings for her were powerful and complicated and put him at her mercy.

Saying *I love you* might make it true.

After he'd hung up the phone, Reeves made a call to a pharmacy and arranged for Bill Wade's prescriptions to be filled and charged to him.

All told, it had been less than a five-minute delay. "Sorry," he apologized to Olivia, rejoining her in the foyer. "That was something of an emergency situation."

Her smile and manner were reserved. "I didn't realize that attorneys, like doctors, are on call during weekends. That will change, I suppose, when you have a different kind of law practice with Duplantis & Duplantis."

"No, it wouldn't necessarily change that much," Reeves replied, perceiving the implied criticism of his kind of law practice. "Attorneys aren't like bankers, conducting business during office hours, unless they specialize in some dull field, like real-estate closings."

"You give out your home number to all your clients?"

"It's printed on my business card." He smiled wryly. "My clients soon learn to call me at my office on a weekend, as well as on weekdays. I'm usually there, not home. This weekend you've wrecked my workaholic habits."

Reeves ushered her through the door into the corridor, thinking that he'd steered them away from the subject. But apparently he hadn't.

"What happens to your cases that you have now when you move to the offices of Duplantis & Duplantis?" she asked. "You won't handle those same kinds of cases, will you?"

"I hope I didn't give you the impression I'm definitely joining the Duplantis firm." Obviously he must have, for she seemed to be making the assumption. "The offer is still on the table. As for my cases that I'm already handling, I'm bound by ethics and conscience to see to the interests of those clients. I can't just drop them."

"No, of course not. Can you refer them over to other plaintiff attorneys?"

"If the client agrees. I signed a contract in good faith, and he or she might decide to hold me to it." Reeves hesitated. "At the risk of sounding conceited, there is also the possibility that I don't know of another attorney who, in my opinion, can handle a particular case as well as I can handle it." A case in point being the Bella malpractice lawsuit, he reflected, with an inner sigh.

They had emerged from the mansion. Her modest compact car, parked in the visitors' parking area, was in view in the foreground. Also in sight was the carriage house where he'd grown up, the son of servants.

"When do you have to give Duplantis & Duplantis your answer?" she inquired.

"There was no deadline stipulated. But I'll need to give them a yes or no soon."

"Are you leaning more in one direction than another?"

At the moment he was leaning in the yes direction because of her. It mattered that she would admire him more as an attorney if he were a member of a prestigious firm.

"I vacillate," he said. "Shall we take your car or mine?"

NO RISK, NO OBLIGATION TO BUY…NOW OR EVER!

GUARANTEED

PLAY "ROLL A DOUBLE" AND GET AS MANY AS FIVE GIFTS!

HERE'S HOW TO PLAY:

1. Peel off label from front cover. Place it in space provided at right. With a coin, carefully scratch off the silver dice. This makes you eligible to receive two or more free books, and possibly another gift, depending on what is revealed beneath the scratch-off area.

2. You'll receive brand-new Silhouette Special Edition® novels. When you return this card, we'll rush you the books and gift you qualify for ABSOLUTELY FREE!

3. Then, if we don't hear from you, every month we'll send you 6 additional novels to read and enjoy months before they are available in stores. You can return them and owe nothing, but if you decide to keep them, you'll pay only $2.71* each plus 25¢ delivery and applicable sales tax, if any*. That's the complete price, and—compared to cover prices of $3.39 each in stores—quite a bargain!

4. When you subscribe to the Silhouette Reader Service™, you'll also get our newsletter, as well as additional free gifts from time to time.

5. You must be completely satisfied. You may cancel at any time simply by sending us a note or a shipping statement marked "cancel" or by returning any shipment to us at our expense.

This lovely heart-shaped box is richly detailed with cut-glass decorations, perfect for holding a precious memento or keepsake—and it's yours absolutely free when you accept our no-risk offer.

SILHOUETTE "NO RISK" GUARANTEE

- You're not required to buy a single book—ever!
- You must be completely satisfied or you may cancel at any time simply by sending us a note or shipping statement marked "cancel" or by returning any shipment to us at our cost. Either way, you will receive no more books; you'll have no obligation to buy.
- The free books and gift you claimed on this "Roll A Double" offer remain yours to keep no matter what you decide.

If offer card is missing, please write to: Silhouette Reader Service, 3010 Walden Ave., P.O. Box 1867, Buffalo, NY 14269-1867

DETACH AND MAIL CARD TODAY!

BUSINESS REPLY MAIL
FIRST CLASS MAIL   PERMIT NO. 717   BUFFALO, NY

POSTAGE WILL BE PAID BY ADDRESSEE

SILHOUETTE READER SERVICE
3010 WALDEN AVE
PO BOX 1867
BUFFALO NY 14240-9952

NO POSTAGE
NECESSARY
IF MAILED
IN THE
UNITED STATES

"Your car," she voted promptly.

"Would you like to drive?"

She smiled and declined graciously. "Thank you, no. I'm happy today to be your passenger."

On the drive to the French Quarter, they recaptured the casual intimacy that had been shattered by the phone call.

Glancing over at her, Reeves felt like bursting into song, like some actor in a romantic musical. He was grinning from ear to ear. The urge to touch her made him reach over at frequent intervals to squeeze her hand or graze his knuckles against her cheek. Braking for a red light, he kissed her.

During the kiss her hand came to rest on his thigh and stayed there. With the light pressure, she laid claim to his whole body.

"What a perfect day!" Her voice had a lilt. "April is probably my favorite month of the year."

"Mine, too."

"The weather is warm and yet not hot."

"You can actually enjoy being out-of-doors."

The two of them in perfect accord, she smiled at him, and he grinned back at her, conscious of how damned good he felt.

His brunch reservations were at the ground-level restaurant in one of the older elegant hotels in the French Quarter. Mentally, Reeves patted himself on the back for having had the forethought to request a table in the restaurant's courtyard, a fact he didn't divulge.

Olivia was delighted when, with typical pomp and ceremony, the maitre d' led them through the crowded main dining room into the courtyard.

"How *perfect!*" she pronounced, gracefully taking a seat at the wrought-iron table, draped in white linen and set with heavy, ornate silverware and stemmed glasses. In the dappled sunshine, the tropical plants and trees growing in profusion in the courtyard were lush green. The lulling sound of water splashing in a fountain could be heard over the quiet voices and laughter of the other diners.

Reeves could only agree that indeed time and place and circumstances were *perfect*, leaving nothing to be desired.

They ordered Bloody Marys and didn't have to wait long before the waiter served the tangy tomato-juice cocktails. Reeves's mouth watered with anticipation as he squeezed a wedge of lime and stirred with a stalk of celery while Olivia did the same. He took his first sip along with her. Not surprisingly, it was the best damned Bloody Mary he'd ever tasted.

Olivia smacked her lips daintily. "Just the right amount of Tabasco sauce."

"And not too heavy on the Worcestershire."

He took a bite of celery and crunched. She followed suit. Celery had never been crisper or more flavorful.

Featured on the brunch menu were crepes with various fillings. They ordered the chef's specialty, with a delicate, rich shrimp-and-crabmeat filling. Reeves savored every mouthful, laying down his fork to butter hunks of hot crusty French bread. Olivia consumed her food with less gusto but with enjoyment. Their waiter kept their champagne glasses full of bubbly golden liquid.

In each glass was a plump red strawberry. While they were waiting for dessert, fresh fruit compote and crepes suzette, Olivia fished out her strawberry, using a teaspoon, held it by the leafy fringe at the stem and ate it. Reeves fished his out and bit off half. Then he fed the rest to her, chewing his portion when she chewed hers, sharing the sweet fruity taste with her.

Earlier he had hitched his chair closer to hers. Now he brought it closer still so that they sat side by side, knees touching under the tablecloth. Even the scrape of metal chair legs on brick struck his ears as a pleasant sound. Closely attuned to her every reaction, he noticed that she didn't wince.

She leaned slightly toward him, as though yielding to the same magnetic attraction that made him want to occupy her space, and confided, "I feel positively *dreamy*. The champagne must be going to my head."

Reeves picked up her glass and held it to her lips. She tilted back her head and swallowed. Then she smiled at him, her lips moist. He picked up his glass and gulped down the rest of the contents to drown the words *I love you*, on the tip of his tongue.

The waiter came to his rescue, commanding their attention while he performed the table-side ceremony of flaming their crepes suzette before serving them.

With the dessert course, they had coffee. It was New Orleans coffee, poured in a thick, coal-black stream from the spout of the silver coffeepot. Contrary to his true preference, Reeves drank his unsweetened and undiluted with heavy cream. Taking a big swallow, he held the strong, bitter brew in his mouth for an extra second or two.

The taste made him grimace, but it wasn't nasty. Even black-and-bitter coffee gave him pleasure today in her company.

Leaving the restaurant, Reeves reached for her hand and was absurdly pleased that she was reaching for his. Numerous times he had walked along this same narrow French Quarter street, seeing the same sights, hearing the same sounds, smelling the same smells. Yet today he might have been a tourist, so novel and fresh was the experience of strolling hand in hand with her and gazing upward at lacy wrought-iron balconies overflowing with plants, the clip-clopping of hooves and jangle of harness growing louder when a mule-drawn carriage passed, leaving behind a pungent barnyard scent.

From all appearances, she was equally intrigued with the familiar quaintness, the distinctive architecture, the foreign flavor, the historic atmosphere. Like Reeves she undoubtedly knew much of the history of the Vieux Carré, the story of how the French and Spanish cultures had blended to form a Creole culture. Undoubtedly she, too, on frequent occasions had visited friends living in French Quarter houses or apartments, but her glance was as avidly curious as his own when occasionally they were treated to glimpses of private bricked courtyards with antique fountains and cool tropical greenery.

The average visitor to New Orleans, Reeves knew, was under the wrong impression that the French Quarter was primarily a tourist mecca and comprised of striptease clubs, jazz halls, a host of antique shops, restaurants and hotels. But actually the majority of the Vieux Carré was residential. Even in the commercial section it wasn't uncommon for apartments to be located in upper stories of the steep shuttered buildings crowding the sidewalks.

"Have you lived in the French Quarter?" Olivia asked, interest in her voice.

"No, I never have. I looked at an apartment once, but it was the typical situation with no reserved parking."

She nodded. "You come home late at night and might have to park your car blocks away on the street."

"At the time I wasn't driving a Porsche, but I was driving an older Ford Mustang that would catch the eye of a professional car thief. Plus I was fond of my stereo, which I'd installed myself."

"Did you? That was clever."

"Not really," he demurred. "It was a matter of economics. For a lot of years I was my own mechanic and grease monkey."

"When I have to take my car in for repairs, I wish I knew more about automobile engines and transmissions and such things. Like most women I have to take on faith whatever the mechanic tells me is wrong."

"Since auto mechanics are men, you can probably smile and get a major engine overhaul at a discount," Reeves teased, squeezing her hand.

Talking, smiling, immersed in each other, they walked on Royal Street, on Bourbon, on connecting streets such as St. Peter, their route meandering. For no particular reason they skirted Jackson Square, where the famous equestrian statue of General Jackson gazed from a lofty height toward the Mississippi River, at his back the tri-steepled facade of St. Louis Cathedral and to right and left, flanking the square on either side, the historic Pontalba apartment buildings.

Eventually Reeves steered Olivia around a corner in the direction of Decatur Street. Reaching Decatur, they veered right again and were headed toward Jackson Square.

"I almost wish I were hungry," she commented when they paused to peer in the store windows of the old Central Grocery store, renowned for its Muffaleta sandwiches and the fascinating inventory of food supplies crowding every inch of shelves from floor to ceiling and also taking up much of the available floor space.

"In an hour or two we should have worked up enough hunger to split a Muffaleta," Reese replied, complacency in his tone. He had no reason to suspect that the whole rest of the afternoon wouldn't unfold in the same leisurely, enjoyable manner.

Everywhere in sight were postcard scenes and historic landmarks. On the opposite side of Decatur was the French Market and Café du Monde, the latter doing its usual round-the-clock business, serving café au lait, coffee laced with hot milk, and beignets, deep-fried pastries dusted with powdered sugar. Up ahead the mule-drawn carriages were pulled up along Jackson Square.

At the corner across from Café du Monde, Reeves pulled Olivia to a stop. "Would you like to cross here and go over to the Moon Walk?" he asked.

Beyond the high levee blocking their view of the Mississippi River was a pleasant promenade with benches for sitting and watching ships passing on the broad, deep, muddy river. It was common knowledge to both of them that the Moon Walk was named after a former mayor of New Orleans, Moon Landrieu.

Olivia deliberated briefly. "Why don't we walk around the square first and see the street entertainers? There seems to be quite a crowd in front of the cathedral."

On three sides of Jackson Square, the streets were pedestrian thoroughfares. Portrait artists were set up along the wrought-iron fence, and roving vendors sold souvenirs and balloons. Musicians and jugglers and other itinerant entertainers used the streets as an impromptu stage.

"Okay." Reeves good-naturedly agreed to her alternative suggestion. A few minutes later he realized how badly he had erred in indulging her impulse rather than his.

"It looks like some kind of protest rally." Olivia stated the obvious when they were close enough to see that the focus of interest was a group of people all wearing identical T- shirts and carrying signs. She read aloud the slogan on a sign. Feed The Hungry Children In The World. "That's certainly a worthwhile cause to draw attention to. I hate to think of anyone, especially little children, going hungry."

Reeves didn't answer. He had spotted a TV Minicam and identified the logo. His sister, Doreen, was an investigative reporter for the same local television station. A protest rally was her type of story.

"What's wrong?" Olivia asked, glancing up at him. "You're cutting off circulation in my hand."

He loosened his hard grip. "Sorry. Let's just get the hell out of here."

"There's no danger of violence. It's a peaceful demonstration," she pointed out. "From the looks of things, they're dispersing anyway."

The Minicam, hoisted on a male shoulder, was moving rapidly toward them. Olivia followed Reeves's glance. Her fingers, intertwined with his, went lax, as she gazed at the Minicam, her face going pale.

"Let's hurry up and go," he urged, dropping her hand to wrap his arm around her slim shoulders.

"No." She resisted his gentle effort to turn her around. Standing erect, she planted her feet on the cobblestones. "I'm not avoiding anyone."

Reeves muttered a curse and almost immediately caught sight of Doreen, striding alongside the cameraman. Under any other circumstances, he would welcome running into his liberal journalist sister. The two of them traveled in different circles, busy with their own careers. When they got together, they disagreed about most things and were outspokenly critical of one another's professions. Her friends weren't his type and vice versa. Still she adored him, and he had a brother's deep affection for her.

Now she had caught sight of him. Raising an arm in the air, she waved exuberantly, a broad smile breaking out.

"Hey, big brother!" she greeted him when she was several yards away. "Fancy seeing you at the scene of a demonstration. Are you scouting out a million-dollar lawsuit?" She grinned at her bearded colleague. "Jack, you got any film left? Shoot some footage of my conservative brother's handsome mug. We'll give him some free advertisement on the ten o'clock news."

"Hi, Doreen."

Her eyebrows lifted at his sober greeting. Several people moved aside to clear a space for her and the cameraman. Up until then she hadn't noticed Olivia. Blank surprise flashed over her features along with appalled recognition. Her welcoming smile turned into a sneer.

"Well, well, well. When did you two turn into an item?" she demanded. Beneath the heavy sarcasm was a note of accusation aimed at Reeves.

"Obviously you haven't been keeping up with the society news," he said gruffly. "Olivia and I had our picture in the newspaper a couple of weeks ago."

His sympathy for his sister only increased his general annoyance and frustration. He could appreciate what an unpleasant shock this was for her, seeing him and Olivia together. In her mind, it was betrayal.

"No, I don't usually open that section of the newspaper. I use it to line my kitty's litter pan."

"Hello, Doreen." Olivia spoke up in a proud, dignified voice, calling attention to herself.

"Hello, Olivia. I see you still have that uptown-New-Orleans-old-money snootiness," his sister observed with snide candor.

"I don't see how that's possible, Doreen. I haven't lived in uptown New Orleans for a number of years."

"And where do you live these days, pray tell?"

"I live in Metairie."

"'Metairie'?" Doreen mocked in disbelief. "You have to be putting me on!"

"No, I'm not putting you on. I work and live in Metairie."

"Doreen, don't let us hold you up," Reeves put in sternly. For all Olivia's poise, he could feel her trembling.

"In other words, get lost. Huh, big brother? This is just too Freudian! First you take up residence in the Prescott mansion. Then you go courting the beautiful little princess who used to live in the mansion, all grown-up and living in Metairie. And conveniently reduced to middle-class status, I'm assuming."

"That's enough, Doreen."

"You assume right," Olivia said.

Olivia was stylish and elegant in comparison to his sister, who wore her straight brown hair cropped short and was dressed in her usual unflattering clothes. Today Doreen wore shapeless black trousers and a mustard-colored jacket. Her makeup was carelessly applied. It had always seemed to Reeves that she perversely emphasized her lack of natural beauty instead of trying to be attractive.

He wanted to shake his sister, but at the same time, he felt sorry for her because he understood so well her cattiness toward Olivia. Underneath Doreen's hard-shelled veneer was a vulnerable, homely, jealous little girl. It didn't help things one bit that Olivia's misfortunes hadn't diminished her beauty.

The cameraman had been standing by quietly. Doreen glanced at him, as though suddenly remembering that he was there. "Poor baby," she commiserated with flip, but sincere apology. "You must be about to drop, lugging that camera. Why don't you go on to the van, and I'll be along? First, let me introduce you to my brother. Jack Zachery. Reeves Talbot."

Reeves and the bearded man, who was attired casually in jeans and a T-shirt, acknowledged the introduction. Reeves then took it upon himself to introduce Olivia to Jack. After Jack had nodded to her politely, he excused himself and moved on.

After he had gone, Doreen surveyed Reeves and Olivia, standing side by side. She shook her head with a kind of bitter bewilderment. "You make a handsome couple. There's no disputing that. What do our parents think about this matchup, big brother? Or haven't you told them about your romance? I see by your expression that you haven't. Always the dutiful son, Reeves calls Mum and Dad once a week," she added for Olivia's information. "I get most of my news about him secondhand from them. They live in Florida, in case you're interested."

"I know that your parents live in Florida. It pleases me very much that they've acclimated so well and are happy," Olivia said.

"Isn't that a *noble* attitude!" Doreen jeered. "How do you feel about having Esther and Charles as your in-laws? And yours truly as your sister-in-law?'' She shuddered with revulsion. ''What a cruel trick of fate this could be. It's like a soap opera script! A farcical comedy of manners! God must be punishing me for all my sins. I've been bad, but not *this* bad!''

''Doreen, shut up,'' Reeves ordered furiously. ''You're making a damned spectacle of yourself! You make me ashamed—'' He broke off, cursing under his breath, as her intelligent brown eyes swam behind tears, and her mouth quivered with hurt.

''I guess I just haven't risen above my lowly origins like you have, Reeves,'' she retorted with husky bitterness. ''I haven't elevated myself from the servants' quarters into the mansion. Forgive me for losing my cool and reacting in an honest fashion. I suspect I've always been an embarrassment. Well, I can do this much for you. I promise that I won't come to the wedding even if I get an invitation. Now I'll leave you two lovebirds to coo at one another.''

She strode past them without telling Reeves goodbye, leaving him to deal with the wreckage of the wonderful day. His shoulders sagged with the enormous relief of having the ghastly scene end.

''Damn, I'm sorry...'' He was apologizing to air.

Olivia had pulled free of his hand and was walking fast away from him. He muttered a violent curse under his breath as he hurried to catch up with her.

''Please, just leave me alone!'' she choked out, and jerked against his hold when he clasped her arm.

He dropped his hand, urging, ''Slow down. Doreen's gone. It's all over.''

''She's a *horrible* person! And she's your *sister!* You're her *brother!*''

Reeves sighed, more discouraged than he'd ever felt in his life. "You bring out the worst side of her, Olivia. You always did. Please slow down, and let's talk about it. You're going to fall and hurt yourself."

"Then you could bring a lawsuit against the city for me and earn a big fee that you could use to furnish and decorate your condominium. Maybe you could buy some of the original furnishings that were sold at auction."

With the scathing outburst, she checked her pace, her steps suddenly lagging. "I shouldn't have said that," she apologized dully. "I was taking my anger at Doreen out on you."

"Believe me when I say I have no desire to own a stick of your grandparents' furniture," he stated, sounding as deeply offended as he was.

"No, I guess not," she said quietly. "You obviously didn't like my grandparents or regard them with any respect."

"No, I didn't *like* them, but I *never* showed them any disrespect. I never spoke the first rude word to either one of them. I was always polite."

"You knew them both your whole life and couldn't be bothered to attend their funeral services."

Reeves was as surprised as he was guiltily defensive. "You noticed that I wasn't there?"

"Yes, I noticed."

He sighed. "It would have been hypocritical of me to go, especially back then. I had no fondness for them. They didn't show any personal interest in Doreen or me. We were their servants' children, and that was the extent of it. Your grandfather was a big contributor to the scholarship funds, yet he didn't offer a red cent toward my college education or toward Doreen's. It's no thanks to him that we both have degrees.''

''He gave you plenty of part-time employment.''

''Yes, he did do that,'' Reeves agreed somberly. ''And he paid me the going wages.''

They walked along in heavy silence, evidently headed back to where his car was parked.

''At the time your grandparents passed away, it would never have occurred to me that my absence at their funerals would be noticed by you,'' he remarked apologetically.

What small hope there was that they might continue their relationship rested somehow in the fact that she *had* noticed in the midst of her grief and loss.

But then she asked with a kind of sad pride, ''Would you have come for my sake?''

''How can I answer that now? All I can honestly say is I *wish* like hell that I had gone. We can't undo the past, Olivia.''

''No, we can't undo the past.''

And the past loomed between them, like a thick plate-glass barrier. Reeves could see her, admire her, feel compassion for her as she walked along beside him, pale and composed after the ordeal of confronting his sister, but he couldn't reach over and make physical contact.

The same old restriction that had hampered them from being friends as children or boyfriend and girl-friend still applied: *Look, but don't touch.*

Chapter Eight

"Let's go somewhere and sit down and talk," Reeves urged.

His note of discouragement deepened Olivia's own dull sense of hopelessness. She felt bruised and shaken after the scene at Jackson Square. Also terribly *alone*— the outsider.

Reeves had rallied to her defense when she was under attack by his sister, but his sympathies had been divided. Olivia had sensed that, heard it in his voice. The blood tie was strong. Come what may, he and Doreen were siblings, part of a family.

"I don't really feel like talking," she replied. "Nothing that we can say can change anything."

"Not things that have already happened. I can't ever undo the fact that I didn't attend your grandparents' funerals."

"And Doreen will always be your sister. Along with all the other degrading emotions that I felt back there, I was envious because no matter how spiteful a person she is, she can count on your brotherly affection and loyalty."

"Doreen isn't a bad person. Because I *am* her brother and grew up with her, I know she has a lot of good qualities."

"She's never shown any of them to me."

"That's because she's always been so envious of you. In her eyes you had everything given to you. Not just the things money can buy, but you were born beautiful. And she was a homely little girl. I think that was the inequity she couldn't forgive you."

"I was also born an only child and didn't know my parents. I thought she was the lucky one, having a brother. I have this vivid picture in my mind of you walking beside her and holding her hand. You played with her, and you would never so much as toss a ball back and forth with me."

"Entertaining my little sister was part of my family role. Our mother worked full-time, even if she was on the premises."

"She brought Doreen over with her when she was a preschooler. I remember that."

"Yes. She cared for me on the job before I entered kindergarten, too. But we weren't allowed the run of the mansion. It was impressed upon us that we had to be on good behavior and stay within our boundaries."

"My grandmother always treated Esther with respect. I often overheard them carrying on conversation."

"My mother liked your grandmother," he conceded.

"Did she like me?" Olivia asked, hearing her own forlorn note. "She was always very kind to me. So was Charles."

"They both considered you their little American princess that they were pleased to care for. My parents' attitude was undoubtedly part of the problem. It had a lot to do with being English and regarding domestic service as a kind of calling. Because they had no class resentments, maybe that fostered stronger resentments in Doreen and me, both of us born here in the United States and growing up with an American perspective."

"None of all that was my doing. And yet I had to suffer the brunt of your and Doreen's unfriendliness."

He went on, obviously striving to be truthful and objective and yet conciliatory. "Your grandparents established a whole set of unwritten rules. My parents helped to enforce them. You and I and Doreen were given our roles. The three of use weren't equals. Blame your grandparents. Blame my parents. Doreen and I just dealt with the situation the only way that we could and salvage our self-esteem."

"What you're saying does help me to understand better."

But the candid discussion didn't narrow the wide gulf between them as they walked along the same French Quarter streets they'd walked along earlier, holding hands. It didn't alleviate any of the disappointment or form a new basis on which they might build a relationship.

"I wish that demonstration had been staged somewhere else. *Anywhere* else," Reeves said, his hands jammed deep into his trouser pockets. "Damn it, if I'd only *insisted* on going to the Moon Walk, we would still be having a great day together."

"This was painful, but it's just as well that it happened before we got any more involved with each other."

"I suppose you're going to ask me not to call or try to see you."

"Don't you honestly think that would be wise?"

"Probably," he concurred bleakly.

On the ride back to his condominium, Olivia stared out the side window of the Porsche, her head throbbing with a dull headache. After today there would be still another reason to avoid St. Charles Avenue, she reflected. The sight of her old home would touch off new heartache. New loss.

"Will you come in?" he asked as they got out of his car. "I have a bottle of wine chilled. Or I could make some coffee."

"No, I really need to be alone, Reeves. Today has stirred up so many bad memories, old ghosts that I'd thought I laid to rest."

"I'm so sorry, Olivia. I'm sorry that you were put through the unpleasantness today. I'm sorry years after the fact for what you went through when Doreen went public with the story about your grandfather."

His guilty note struck her as odd.

"I got through it."

They walked to her car. She took out her keys and handed them to him when he held out his hand. He unlocked her door and opened it for her.

"Did you know about Doreen's investigation ahead of time?" she asked.

Reeves nodded. "Some months ahead of time."

The faintly guilty note was in his voice again, mixed in with sincere apology.

Olivia glanced across the flagstone pavement toward the building that had originally been a carriage house, then later servants' quarters where he'd grown up and now was expensive residential property. "I don't suppose it even crossed your mind to give me some forewarning," she said, something niggling at the back of her mind.

He sighed. "Actually I knew that day I ran into you on the LSUNO campus. Doreen had told me about her investigation in confidence."

"You knew that day, and you didn't breathe a word of it. You didn't give me any advance warning that my grandfather's name and reputation were going to be crucified in the local media." Olivia gazed at him accusingly, slowly shaking her head.

"I felt compassion for you, Olivia. But look at the position I was in," Reeves implored. "Doreen had sworn me to secrecy."

"Telling me would hardly have amounted to leaking her story. I certainly didn't have any contacts with the press, other than the editors of society columns."

"I should have said something," he admitted. "But I didn't. That day I had just gotten news that I'd passed the bar. I was on cloud nine. Also, if you recall, you gave me the brush-off. All those things are no excuse, I realize. Can you forgive me?"

"I'm not that big a person, Reeves. Even if I could forgive you, I couldn't forget. Before we make any more revelations, please, let's just say goodbye," she begged him bitterly, getting into her car. With hands that trembled, she managed to fasten her seat belt.

He leaned down. "Please, Olivia, don't leave like this. You're too upset to drive."

"I'm too upset to stay." The key finally inserted in the ignition, she started the car. "Once I'm on the interstate, I'll be fine. I'm going to be fine, Reeves. You take care.''

He straightened, closed the car door and stepped back. Her vision blurred by tears, Olivia glanced in her rearview mirror before she pulled out onto the street and saw him standing there, watching her depart. It seemed an additional cause for sorrow that her last view of him was so distorted.

The apartment was dead quiet. Judy had gone for the day to visit her family. Olivia leaned against the door, dreading the absolute privacy in her apartment mate's absence. There was nothing to protect her from memories. Nothing to prevent her from turning the pages of photo albums and scrapbooks.

The painful nostalgia of all those old memories would have a new razor's edge because of today and because of Reeves. There was an added dimension of loss, disillusionment and grief because of him.

When the phone rang hours later, it was evening, and she was drained from the emotional rigors of lonely reminiscence, her face stiff from the cleansing bath of tears that had flowed. Sitting in bed, she held an album on her lap, open to a studio portrait of her grandfather.

Reaching to pick up the receiver, she was expecting the caller to be Judy, who hadn't returned. Often her apartment mate ended up spending the night in Ponchatoula when she visited on a Sunday.

"Hello." Olivia's voice came out husky and sad.

"Hi. I had to call and make sure you were okay."

Reeves's deep, concerned voice was in her ear, not Judy's voice. Against all logic and experience, she was comforted by the sound.

"I'm okay," she assured him.

"Is Judy there with you?"

"No. She's visiting her family in Ponchatoula. When the phone rang, I was expecting it to be her."

Olivia should reprimand him for calling her. She should cut the call short. But only the comprehension of what she *should* do was there, not the motivation.

"You've been crying," he stated with gruff sympathy.

She cleared her throat. "Yes. But the crying helped."

"I could never stand to see you cry."

His words vividly brought back a forgotten scene from their childhood, one the camera hadn't captured. She couldn't have been more than six or seven years old and had fallen and hurt herself. He'd picked her up and held and comforted her.

"What are you doing?" he asked, and the tender, gruff tone of the man echoed the young boy's tone.

"I'm sitting in bed where I've been for hours, looking at photo albums and scrapbooks. I came across a few pictures of you and Doreen and—your parents." It had been on the tip of her tongue to call the couple Esther and Charles. "As I was looking at a family picture of the four of you, a thought occurred to me. I'll bet it offended you and Doreen that I called your parents by their first names."

"It did," he admitted. "I'm surprised you've kept pictures that included Doreen and me. I'm surprised you didn't cut us both up in little pieces long ago as a symbolic gesture."

"These albums were the bulk of my inheritance," she replied. "Are you at home?"

"No, I'm at my office. I've been trying without any success to get some work done. I keep going over today in my mind, replaying conversations."

"None of what happened was really your fault. Or my fault. Or even Doreen's fault. Given all the background and the personalities, it was just destined to play out that way."

"I hate that whole theory, Olivia. The last thing I ever wanted to be was a human pawn. I should have been more in control today," he insisted. "I got overwhelmed and let myself be carried by the tide."

"Well, I don't blame you, Reeves. For any part of the day," she added.

Silent understanding passed between them. She was taking her share of the responsibility for their having made love.

"That part was all wrong, too," he said regretfully. "It wasn't the right time or place. Now there's no undoing it. *Damn*, I feel helpless and angry with myself."

He meant *hopeless*. Olivia didn't want to talk about the error of making love with him or focus in on what a serious mistake it had been.

"When I look back on my whole past history, I feel angry with myself," she confessed. "I wonder if I couldn't have made a difference. It's no excuse that I was oblivious to so much beneath the surface. For example, the thought never once crossed my mind back when you were putting yourself through college that my grandfather could have been helping to finance your education. Is it possible, perhaps, that he might have offered and your parents refused?" Hopefulness was in her voice.

"No, I'm afraid not," he said gently. "We had family forums when my parents discussed asking him."

"You forbade them to," she guessed.

His silence said that he had. "Your grandfather had no obligation toward me or Doreen."

"Charity begins at home, Reeves. As you brought up today, he was a big donor to scholarship funds."

"His rationale will remain a mystery, Olivia. There's probably an explanation. Doreen and I got good educations anyway."

"You're being kind," she accused quietly. "You and I both know the explanation. My grandfather wasn't really the philanthropist he pretended to be. Giving you and Doreen a helping hand wouldn't have bought him any public recognition or any private favors."

"His philanthropy still accomplished some good," he pointed out. "Deserving students got scholarships and hospital wings got built. For all we know, there was some genuine motivation to do good. Your grandfather was certainly very generous to you. And it always seemed to me that he was genuinely devoted to your grandmother."

"I got everything I ever asked for and more. But now I'm not even sure that some of his generosity toward me wasn't for show. He made such a big display of pampering and spoiling me. I would have sworn that he *was* devoted to my grandmother, but then, thanks to Doreen, I learned after he was dead that he'd kept mistresses while he was being a pillar of the church. That's not marital devotion, in my book."

Olivia hadn't intended to pour out her disillusionment, but once she'd started she couldn't seem to stop. She went on, "In the most real sense, I was a poor little rich girl and didn't realize it. My respect and admiration for my grandfather had no basis. It was totally devastating to learn that he wasn't honest and morally upright and honorable, all the things I held him up to be."

And still she couldn't stop. "How can I ever trust any man, if I was wrong to trust my grandfather? How can I trust my instincts about men when I developed them admiring him, blind to his real character? I can't."

"No man—no human being—is without faults, Olivia," Reeves objected, his tone passionate and earnest. "But there are many men in this world who are faithful to their wives. Men who have principles and high ideals and aren't corruptible. You can't condemn us all because your grandfather disappointed you. Some of us deserve a chance to prove that we can be trusted."

"My grandfather isn't the only man I've misjudged. I was taken in by William, too. He'd sworn his undying love and then didn't stand by me. I thought he embodied manliness, and he turned out to be weak when the going got rough."

"What about the other two men you were engaged to later when you were more mature? Did you misjudge them?"

"I think the reason I didn't fall in love with either one of them was I can't trust a man. That truth came to me this afternoon."

He was silent a long moment, as though absorbing her meaning. "Complete trust takes years, Olivia. We all have to go with our instincts and gamble on getting hurt."

"I don't seem to be able to do that, Reeves."

"And it's very unlikely that you would gamble on trusting me. Is that what you're telling me?"

"Don't you feel the same way about me?"

"Whether I can trust you or not, I can't accept the idea of not seeing you," he answered simply. "I'm willing to take the risk that I'll fall seriously in love with you and end up in the same boat with my soul mates, Eric and Sam.''

"Both of whom are happily married," she reminded him with a quiet cynicism. "Shouldn't you get back to work?"

"I should, but I really don't want to."

"Is the case you're working on tonight one that you'll take to court or settle yourself, regardless?" He was slow to reply, so she added, "Regardless of whether you decide to join Duplantis & Duplantis."

His heavy sigh came over the line. "This particular case has turned into a real albatross. After I took it on, a conflict of interest developed. And yet I feel a real responsibility toward the client."

His answer didn't exactly seem like a response to her question.

"How long ago did you take it on?"

"About six weeks ago. Shortly afterward, William Duplantis approached me on behalf of his family firm. Doors that had been closed started to open. I met the Hymers. You came back into my life."

"Where does the conflict of interest come in? Or can you tell me?"

"Not over the phone," he said reluctantly. "Tonight I wouldn't want to discuss it. You're sounding much better, by the way, not so sad and despondent."

"I'm feeling almost back to normal. Thank you for listening. Now I can put away these albums and silly keepsakes for another five or six years."

"Describe some of your keepsakes," he requested.

"You don't really want me to," Olivia demurred.

"Yes, I do."

"Well, there's a label from a bottle of champagne that was smuggled into my Sweet Sixteen birthday party."

"Dom Pérignon."

"Yes, how did you know?"

"You mentioned that night that you were drinking Dom Pérignon."

"That remarkable memory of yours must serve you well as an attorney," she marveled.

"You wore a pretty, sexy red dress with tiny straps," he recalled. "You were lovely and nubile. I couldn't keep my eyes off you."

"You were handsome and dashing in your black slacks and white shirt and red sash."

"It wasn't a shirt. It was more like a woman's blouse. I felt ridiculous with those damned loose sleeves flapping on my arms."

"I was wildly jealous because every time I glanced over at you, you were surrounded by my girlfriends, talking to them, smiling at them."

"Most of the conversation between me and your girlfriends pertained to the concoctions I was mixing for them. None of them could hold a candle to you. But you were too young for me to fool around with, even without all the other taboos."

"After that night, you didn't work any more parties for my grandparents, did you?"

"No. I kept my distance from you after that night. What are some of the other souvenirs you've kept?" he asked, moving them on to a safer reminiscence.

"Let's see. Here's an invitation to a debutante tea."

"Read it."

"No!"

"Come on."

She humored him and at his urging flipped through the pages of scrapbooks and described sentimental items. It was surprisingly easy and natural to recount events to him and share anecdotes, some embarrassing and some amusing. His comments and responses conveyed a warm interest.

When he chuckled at an episode, Olivia found herself laughing along with him. It seemed no less than a miracle that she would feel like laughing tonight.

"I would never have believed I'd be telling you all this," she said. "You must really be in a mood to procrastinate."

"I only wish you were showing me your scrapbooks," he replied softly.

Olivia imagined him there, sitting next to her on the bed, looking at the pages with her. She closed her eyes, suppressing a deep surge of longing. Closing the scrapbook on her lap, she put it aside, glancing at the clock.

"We've been on the phone more than an hour. It's time for me to put this stuff away and let you work on your albatross case."

"When you go to bed, I'll probably still be here, burning the midnight oil."

"You got that far behind taking off yesterday afternoon and today?"

"My aim is not just to catch up, but to get ahead of the game," he explained. "Tomorrow night I'd like very much to see you."

Olivia waited for a specific invitation, but none came. *Would she like to see him?* was the question he asked silently, hopefully.

"What do you have in mind, Reeves?"

"Picking you up early and taking you home as late as possible and spending the time in between together. Beyond that, I have no plan."

He wasn't expecting her to spend the night with him at his condo.

"I like to be home at a reasonably early hour on a weeknight. I can come home and change and be ready by six."

"I'll be there at six," he promised.

From his tone he might have been making a more serious commitment.

After telling him goodbye and hanging up, Olivia opened up one of the photo albums to the studio portrait of her grandfather. She gazed at it a long moment, then collected all the albums and scrapbooks and put them away in her closet.

In his office on Gravier Street, Reeves gently replaced the receiver. He sat for a long moment, his head in his hands, pondering what to do about the Bella lawsuit.

Sissy Bella was associated with many of Olivia's happy memories. Time and again Olivia had mentioned her tonight, relating anecdotes. How could he handle a malpractice case against Dr. Bella and still date Olivia? He *couldn't*.

Other attorneys in New Orleans besides himself had won malpractice cases. Among them, he had the highest regard for a woman attorney named Brenda Quinn. His reluctance to hand Bill Wade's lawsuit against Bella over to her might be nothing more than his ego talking. She might be every bit as capable as Reeves.

He could go ahead and take the deposition himself and prepare the case. Then when he approached Bill Wade and his wife about changing attorneys, he could honestly give them his assurance that all the preliminary ground work had been carefully done for bringing the case before a jury.

In the meanwhile his conscience would just have to bother him because of the duplicity. He didn't dare be up-front with Olivia and explain to her his professional dilemma. He felt on such fragile footing with her.

Her tendency would naturally be to give Dr. Bella every benefit of the doubt. She wouldn't want to listen to all the grim details of the case, and Reeves didn't want to be the one to force her to hear them. He hated to tear down her high regard for Dr. Bella. She'd been through so much disillusionment already. He wished she didn't even have to know.

She probably wouldn't know if the case were quietly settled. But then Bella would keep on operating. *Damn,* what a complicated mess!

Reese couldn't dwell on those complications tonight. He was still Bill Wade's attorney and needed to focus his legal mind on planning the depositions he would be taking in the next couple of weeks.

Tonight he had to clear his head of thoughts of Olivia and table the urge she brought out in him to lay the world at her feet and make up to her for every misfortune.

Chapter Nine

Through the open door of his office, Reeves could hear Alan Cramer bantering with Joan. He stood up, stretching, ready to take a short break. His day had begun early in the predawn hours, like all his days began now.

The old cliché about there not being enough hours in a twenty-four-hour day had never been more true for Reeves than in the past three weeks. He refused to let a backlog of work build up, but he also refused to let his law practice interfere with spending evenings and weekends with Olivia.

It meant packing his schedule full and sharpening his concentration. Reeves had shifted into a higher gear. When he went into court for a trial or negotiated for a big settlement with a team of high-powered attorneys, he was almost inspired, like an athlete who moved into an upper sphere of performance under the pressure of competition.

Reeves had exceptional athletic ability. In high school he had been scouted by college football coaches in other states, but he had chosen not to go the football-scholarship route. He didn't love the sport of football enough to put himself heart and soul into being a football jock. Brute force was too much an element of winning and losing, for his liking, and he had concluded by the end of his senior year in high school that it was rather senseless to punish his body and possibly incur permanent injuries.

The sport that Reeves really loved was tennis. He hadn't taken it up until he was in college. It was an upper-class sport and hadn't been taught in his physical education classes in high school. None of his friends had played it.

He'd become a tennis fanatic almost immediately upon picking up a racket. The game had come easily to him. The coach of the tennis team had observed him playing a match and had approached him with the suggestion that he might try out for the team the following year, if he was willing to invest some money in lessons from a pro and devote a great deal of time to practice.

Reeves, of course, hadn't had the money or the time to spare. He had scheduled tennis permanently into his busy life, though. He'd read all of the books in the library written by various tennis greats and watched televised coverage of famous tournaments such as Wimbledon. He'd managed to play often, having no shortage of opponents, including some of his professors. Occasionally he'd entered tournaments, but would usually have to default at some stage because his part-time jobs took priority.

During law school, it had been the same story. Once he was practicing law and finally wasn't strapped financially, Reeves had joined the Hilton River Center, an excellent indoor sports facility with tennis courts, conveniently located in the downtown business district. There he'd played some of the best men players in the New Orleans area and defeated them more often than not.

He could well afford to join one of the several old, elite country clubs in New Orleans. Whether his membership application would be approved was another matter. The probability that it wouldn't be approved hadn't particularly bothered him. He didn't choose to belong to any organization that excluded people on the basis of race or religion, as the country clubs were known to do.

Or at least he *hadn't* chosen to do so when there was actually no choice to be made. Now he found himself with contacts on membership committees.

Hearing Alan's voice brought tennis to mind. It also brought to mind thoughts of the coming weekend. He and Olivia were invited to be houseguests of the Hymers at their summer home in Pass Christian on the Mississippi Gulf Coast. They would also be mixed doubles partners in a small tournament that apparently was an annual event, played on private courts.

The participants were all members of the Hymers' social circle. William Duplantis and his wife, who also had a summer home in Pass Christian, were cosponsors. Sissy and George DeMarco would be among the Duplantises' houseguests, much to Reeves's discomfort. He was sure to be ill at ease around her. How could he be friendly when, unbeknownst to her, and still unbeknownst to Olivia, he was building a case of malpractice against her father?

Reeves had other reasons to be ambivalent about the weekend. Attending dinner parties or black-tie society affairs and socializing with people like the Hymers and Duplantises for an evening was one thing. Weekending with them was something else. He was feeling some insecurity about getting in over his social depth.

It would have been nice to spend a weekend on the Gulf Coast with just her. But she'd left it up to him whether to accept the invitation, and he'd felt put on the spot. The whole decision had taken on overtones of the weekend's being a social test of some kind, a test he needed to pass to boost his own confidence level with her. There was the nagging possibility that she'd pretended to be neutral about the invitation because of doubts about whether he'd fit in and enjoy himself.

Reeves had accepted. He would provide her with a damned good tennis partner, if nothing else. His confidence wasn't lacking on that score.

"Good morning, Counselor." Alan greeted him from the doorway.

"Just the man I want to see," Reeves said, remaining standing and flexing muscles.

The other attorney turned around in the pretense of leaving. Then, grinning, he strolled over and perched on the arm of the sofa, an indication that his visit would be short. His grin became an amused smirk as he watched Reeves toss an imaginary tennis ball high into the air and go through the athletic motion of a smash serve.

"Fault," Alan said.

"Ace," Reeves corrected. "How about some mixed doubles tonight? I have a court reserved at the River Center. You and Kay against Olivia and me. We need some practice." Briefly he explained about the tournament in Pass Christian that weekend.

Alan shrugged. "Sure. I'll call Kay and set it up for tonight. Do you want to do something as a foursome afterward?" He read Reeves's reaction and supplied his own answer. "No, you want to do something as a twosome with Olivia. Right?"

"Right. Nothing personal."

The sandy-haired man waggled his hand to indicate that no apology was needed. "This could be a real test, you know, the two of you pairing up as tennis partners."

"Not for me," Reeves denied. "She could be the worst tennis partner in the world, and I couldn't care less. The only test is going to be keeping my eye on the tennis ball. The purpose of tonight's practice session is to get some preview of having her on a court with me, dressed in a tennis outfit. I hope I can keep my mind on the game enough to keep score."

Alan shook his head. "I never thought I'd see the day when a woman could be that serious a distraction for you. Is *serious* a key word?"

"It's a key word." Reeves dropped back down into his chair behind his desk.

"Should I be expecting a wedding invitation in due time?"

"Unfortunately not."

Alan cocked an eyebrow at the sober response. His expression was mildly concerned as well as quizzical. "Does that mean I won't be invited?" he asked facetiously.

"You'll be my best man at my wedding, in the event that there ever is one." Reeves sighed. "At the reception you can dance with my sister, that is if your arthritis isn't too advanced and you can stand without your cane. I don't dare get my hopes up by thinking marriage to Olivia, Alan. Right now I'm getting my nerve up to ask her to live with me."

The allusion to Doreen didn't need explanation. Alan knew the background information and was aware of the enmity between Reeves's sister and Olivia.

"She wouldn't exactly be slumming if she moved in with you," Alan commented. "That's a great condo of yours."

"Want to buy it?"

"You serious?" His quick smile was wry. "There's that word, *serious,* again. I would definitely be interested, if you're thinking of selling. Give me first shot."

Reeves named a price.

"Sounds like fair market value," Alan said. "Let me consult with my real-estate expert and review my finances. Where are you planning to move? Out to Metairie?"

"That depends on Olivia. My preference would be to stay in uptown New Orleans, but I would move to Metairie."

"She objects to moving in with you on St. Charles? Too many old associations?"

"I haven't broached the subject. But, yes, there are too many old associations."

Alan nodded. He scratched his head, grimacing. "I hate to mention this option, for selfish reasons. You wouldn't have to sell your condo. You could lease it, with no problems."

Then if Reeves and Olivia parted company, Reeves could move back into his condo. Alan tactfully didn't state the rest of what he was thinking.

Reeves shook his head. "I don't want to own it. I'll never have any desire to live there again."

Alan stood. "Enough said. My conscience is clear. And don't expect any mercy tonight from Kay and me." With a wave of farewell, he ambled out of Reeves's office after establishing the time of the tennis date.

Seconds later Joan breezed in with a stack of transcribed depositions pertaining to the Bella lawsuit.

"After typing these, I may never go under the knife on an operating table," she declared. "Our good doctor knocks his patients out with alcohol fumes. I predict this case will never come to trial. His insurance company will settle. They'll jack up the price of his malpractice coverage. He'll jack up his fees and pass the expense on to his next victims."

"Bella needs to be barred from the operating room, Joan." Reeves riffled the edges of the stack of depositions. "That's the message I'm getting from surgical nurses and hospital personnel and his fellow surgeons, even though no one will state that opinion for the record. He's too important and influential. The case should go to court. It needs to get publicity." He raised his hands and then dropped them. "But Bill Wade and his wife will have to decide whether they'll settle out of court or not."

"You're expecting a big settlement, just like I am," she said wisely. "You're confident that the state medical review panel is going to find negligence."

"Not confident," he objected. "In law you can never afford to count your chickens. But I don't see how the panel can fail to find negligence. Nor in my judgment does it seem that big a gamble to take the case before a jury." Even though he wouldn't be Bill Wade's attorney, Reeves had given a jury trial plenty of thought.

"The plaintiff wouldn't have to be subjected to the ordeal of appearing in court. A video of him at home would show his poor health condition and dependency, his pathetic life quality. Joan, I can't imagine that a jury wouldn't award as much or more compensation than he would get in a settlement. But there are no guarantees."

"You really want to take the case to trial, don't you?"

"I want his attorney to take the case to trial. That attorney isn't going to be me if the Wades agree. I'm hoping to make a present of the lawsuit to a more objective colleague." Reeves disclosed his intention to his secretary.

Joan stared at him, her jaw dropping in disbelief. "Some present. You should make a friend for life."

"I don't know about that, but I can avoid making some enemies and closing some doors. Dr. Bella is a socially prominent man. He has a lot of friends. Bringing a malpractice suit against him isn't going to make me very popular."

"You knew the doctor was New Orleans high society when you took on the case," Joan pointed out not sympathizing in the least.

"Yes, I knew. But some of those doors I mentioned weren't open then." The offer from Duplantis & Duplantis had come shortly afterward, turning out to be a combination social and career package. Falling in love with Olivia had come afterward. He knew without any doubt that he was in love with her.

"Are you saying you wouldn't take the case today?" Joan asked.

Reeves stood and began slipping on his jacket. His answer stuck in his throat. "No, I wouldn't take it."

She shrugged. "In that case, you should give it to another attorney, whether or not the Wades agree. You should tell them plain out that you don't think you can represent them as well as you should.''

"Any mixed feelings I have wouldn't affect the way I represented Bill Wade if I remained his attorney,'' he said, stung by her implied criticism.

Joan didn't back off. "The Wades are typical of many of your clients, Reeves. Not very well-educated. They'll look to you to tell them what to do, whether to settle or hold out and go to trial.''

"I realize that. I realize that they deserve to have an attorney whose only concern is what is best for them. A top-notch attorney.'' Reeves snapped his briefcase closed with more force than was necessary.

His secretary's hard expression softened. "You're due in court in fifteen minutes,'' she reminded him unnecessarily. "Now you can thank me for telling you something else you already know.''

"You're such a hard-boiled individual, Joan, and never let your sympathies get the best of you.'' Reeves touched her shoulder as he strode past her on his way out. "That's what I admire most about you.''

"Yeah,'' she called after him. "And you're one of those ambulance-chasing lawyers without a conscience, out to get rich on other people's misery. That's why I like working for you.''

Reeves had given her a key to his condo. Olivia let herself in, carrying a plastic garment bag and her overnight case. The bag contained her tennis outfit, clothes to wear that evening and a linen suit-dress to wear to work the following morning.

Unbeknownst to Reeves, she had come prepared to spend the night with him for the first time. He'd commented that he wished they could sleep together, but he hadn't actually suggested that she stay overnight at his condo. She assumed that he sensed her reluctance to sleep in the building that had been her old home.

In truth, Olivia continued to feel odd coming there. She thought Reeves might sense that, too, but he hadn't brought up moving again. If he had, she would have agreed. After three weeks of seeing him, she couldn't think in terms of anything but a long-term relationship.

Still she wasn't sure that she would go through with staying overnight. She might very well go back to Metairie, not even mentioning that she'd come prepared.

His condo was clean and neat, as it always seemed to be. He hired a cleaning service that came once a week, and in between, apparently picked up after himself. Entering his bedroom, Olivia saw that the bed was made up. There was a dent in the comforter where he had sat down at the foot of the bed, probably to put on his shoes.

Pausing on her way to his walk-in closet, she put her overnight case down and caressed the spot with her palm. A surge of tender, possessive emotion made her jerk her hand away and stand upright.

Was she falling in love with Reeves?

"I adore him," she said aloud. "He's a nice person and a marvelous companion."

In his large walk-in closet, she found space for her garment bag next to one of his suits. Kicking off her pumps, she dug her toes into the thick carpet and stood there gazing at his clothes and his shoes, one pair of which was white tennis shoes. Giving in to temptation, she stroked a sleeve here, a collar there, knowing that he wouldn't object to her touching his clothes in his absence. The liberty was hers to enjoy.

The phone rang out in the bedroom, startling her. Should she answer it or let his answering machine take the call? she wondered. The caller might be Reeves himself, checking to find out if she'd arrived.

That possibility brought Olivia quickly out of the closet. She scrambled across the king-size bed instead of walking around it and reminded herself of a teenager, grabbing up the receiver. Her hello came out eager and breathless.

"Hi. You're there." Reeves's voice was low and warm. "Did you just walk in and run to catch the phone? You sound out of breath."

"No, I've been here a few minutes. I was poking around in your closet and thinking about you. Will you be here anytime soon?" Olivia blushed at the flagrant invitation in her words.

"I'm on my way. I'm talking to you on the phone in my car. You go back to whatever you were doing and keep those thoughts of me in your head."

"Maybe I'll just lie here on the bed and wait for you."

"You're lying on the bed now?"

"Across it on my stomach. I took a shortcut to get to the phone," she explained. Horns sounded in the background. "Are you stuck in a traffic jam?"

"I was holding up traffic. The light had turned green." A muttered curse.

"What's wrong?"

"Nothing. The car in front of me stopped suddenly."

"You'd better hang up and concentrate on driving. I want you here safe and sound."

"Talk to me. Tell me about your day."

"You wouldn't want to hear about my day."

"Yes, I would," he insisted. "Just omit the parts that will make me jealous, like your male co-workers paying you compliments."

"You've left me with very little to say," Olivia teased. "Let's see. I went shopping on my lunch hour."

"What did you buy?"

"A pair of sandals to wear this weekend."

"I'm sure I'll like them on you."

"How can you be sure?"

"Your painted toenails will show. I'm assuming you won't wear panty hose."

"I won't. Do you have a foot fetish?" she inquired, bending her legs at the knees and kicking her feet.

"With you I have a foot fetish, a leg fetish, an arm fetish, an any-part-of-your-body fetish." There was the sound of horns blaring again.

"Where are you?"

He told her, and it was only minutes away, an intersection on St. Charles.

"I'm going to hang up and take off my panty hose so that you can enjoy some of your fetishes after you've safely arrived," she said.

"Can't you take off your panty hose and talk on the phone?" he cajoled. "I'm managing to drive a car and keep up my end of the conversation."

"Hold on. I'm rolling over on my back. This is quite a trick with one hand. My panties are coming down, too." He swore violently. "Reeves, are you okay?"

"I'm fine, sweetheart. My pants aren't too comfortable, but I'm only a couple of blocks away. How are you coming along with those panty hose?"

"I should have them off and be able to unlock the door for you. Watch out, though, because I may tear off your clothes."

"You have my hopes up."

"Just your hopes? I'm blushing for talking like this," she confessed, her cheeks hot. It wasn't embarrassment, though, making her breasts heavy or causing them to tingle. Just from talking to him on the phone, she was languorous with anticipation, ready for his lovemaking.

"I love it when you're shameless," he declared.

"I never was shameless before."

"No? Tell me more. Swell my ego, not to mention the part of my anatomy I would cover up with a loincloth...."

They didn't hang up until after he had arrived and had parked and turned off the engine. By the time she had gotten to the door, he was on the other side of it, carrying his briefcase in one hand and holding his suit jacket draped in front of him.

"That must be a record!" she marveled. "Did you run?"

"Hell, yes, I ran."

He put his briefcase down, tossed his jacket on top of it, scooped Olivia up in his arms and kicked the door closed, all in one vigorous, athletic motion. She wound her arms around his neck and smiled at him in happy embarrassment.

"Don't turn shy and ladylike on me, sweetheart," he chided. "You've got me worked up to a fever pitch with that telephone foreplay."

"Then take me into the bedroom and ravish me."

"First, how about a welcome-home kiss. I could get used to a reception like this, you know."

She kissed him, her lips soft against the firmness of his. The contact was warm and sweet and then quickly hungry as their mouths parted under harder pressure and their tongues mated.

He carried her into the bedroom while they continued to kiss. When he set her on her feet, Olivia was loosening the knot of his tie. His fingers went immediately to the fastening of her skirt. They undressed each other with a kind of urgent dexterity. The efficiency of Reeves's hands in removing her clothes evoked pleasure as did her own lack of fumbling in unbuttoning his shirt and unzipping his slacks.

It wasn't the first time they'd undressed each other. It wasn't the first time they'd made love. The familiarity didn't lessen the intense delight or the satisfaction.

"That was good for me again, in case you're wondering," she murmured, lying in his close embrace afterward.

He hugged her tighter and said nothing.

"You strictly don't believe in talking, do you?" she remarked.

"Does it bother you?"

"I guess it bothers me a little."

"Did you ever feel that something is beyond your power of words?"

"Lots of things are beyond my power of expression. I'm not nearly as articulate as you are."

"I would need to be a poet to describe the satisfaction I feel after we've made love. It's not just physical, but, well, spiritual. For a short space of time, we might be the only two people in the universe, a small, cozy universe."

Olivia was too touched for words, which meant she *had* to say something. "What a lovely sentiment." She kissed his shoulder.

He went on. "It's not a state of obliviousness. There's this wonderful sense of being suspended in the present. Everything in the past is irrelevant. The future isn't a problem. There's just *now*."

"No wonder you're in no state to talk."

"It's not that I'm in no state to speak," he denied. "I'm just inhibited."

"You like to be in better control of your speech faculty," she suggested.

"Something like that." Olivia could feel a tension in his body. "There's something I want to ask you."

"What is it?"

"Would you consider living with me at some future date? Not immediately. This isn't a proposition that calls for a yes or no now," he assured her.

"I gather not," she said. "I've never had a live-in relationship with a man."

"I haven't lived with a woman, either, but I'd like to live with you."

Evidently it wasn't a burning desire, though.

"Ask me when you're ready, and we'll discuss it. It's not a step that I can take casually." Olivia rolled over onto her back. He propped himself up on his elbow beside her as she continued, "Judy couldn't afford the rent on our apartment. She would get another apartment mate. If our living together didn't work out, there I would be, out in the cold."

While he mulled that over, Olivia flipped the edge of the sheet over her.

"One solution would be for you to keep paying your share of the rent until you felt secure with our living arrangement," he said. "I don't much like the idea, because it would put our arrangement on a trial basis, but I could understand if you wanted to do that."

"If I kept paying rent on my old apartment, I couldn't afford my fair share of our living expenses," she pointed out.

He shrugged. "I'll pay our living expenses."

"In other words, I would be your mistress. No thanks."

He frowned. "Okay, then, you can pay part of the expenses. That can all be worked out. We can prorate a split, based on our incomes. Whatever. I'll sign a contract."

Olivia smiled with grudging amusement. "If that doesn't sound like a lawyer."

She reached and caressed his cheek. He caught her hand and kissed her palm.

"So your reaction to the idea of our living together isn't negative?" he asked.

"No, my reaction isn't negative."

From his expression, Olivia might as well have said yes to a marriage proposal. He squeezed her hand, bent down and kissed her very gently on the lips.

"I can't live in a place with bare walls like this one, though," she said. "I would have to hang some pictures, do some decorating."

"When the time comes, you can have a free hand in decorating. We can buy new furniture, buy some decent artwork, repaint. You can redo the place from top to bottom to suit you." He kissed her again, as though sealing the bargain, and bounded out of the bed energetically. "We'd better get dressed for our tennis date with Alan and Kay. They'll be tough competition. Alan doesn't hit with a lot of pace. He's more of a finesse player and smart as hell...."

Apparently in the best of moods, he had switched his thoughts to tennis and their plans for the evening. The discussion evidently hadn't left him with a nagging dissatisfaction, like she was feeling. There hadn't been any explanation from him of *why* she was the first woman he'd wanted to live with. He hadn't probed into her willingness to have a live-in relationship with him, although she'd left him a wide opening, admitting that she had never been willing before with any other man.

There had been no mention of the word *love.* No hint that he might be contemplating marrying her at some future date, despite all the obstacles, the main one being his sister.

Did she want him to be falling in love with her?

Olivia was deeply disturbed that a clear-cut yes or no didn't form in her head. She tried to match her light mood to his as they donned their tennis clothes, and soon it wasn't necessary to try. The vague depression evaporated into enjoyment of his company.

She *did* adore him. He was so incredibly attractive, tall and well built with broad shoulders and a hard, fit, muscular body without a sign of flab. His voice was wonderful to hear—deep and masculine and resonant. When he laughed his hearty laugh or chuckle in amusement, life seemed a romantic comedy that could only end happily ever after.

She loved the play of expressions on his face that made him that much more handsome. She was impressed by his intelligence. He was highly perceptive. He was highly personable. He was fun. He was interesting. He had depth to his character.

Most important, Olivia's instincts told her that Reeves was decent and honorable. They told her that she *had* found a man she could trust.

But how reliable were those instincts?

Chapter Ten

"I'll have to do something really nice for Judy," Olivia mused. "Bless her, she's stepping into my shoes tomorrow so that my four elderly ladies can have their bridge game and luncheon."

It was Friday afternoon, and she and Reeves were on their way to Pass Christian for the weekend.

"Your Saturday morning social work, as she calls it. What would you have done, if she hadn't agreed to pinch-hit?" he asked.

"I would have gotten someone else."

"Called in a favor?"

She glanced over at him, taken aback by his astuteness. "In a manner of speaking."

Reeves explained. "Judy tagged you as the unofficial Miss Manners among your co-workers. According to her, you're an unpaid social consultant."

"I'm not really!" Olivia scoffed. "I'm just a ready source of information. It's easier to ask someone who might know than to consult a book on social etiquette."

"Reading a how-to book on a subject doesn't instill confidence," he commented. "A library on social etiquette can't substitute for your kind of background."

He sounded admiring.

"What amazes me is that people fret as much as they do about the fine points of etiquette. Traditions are nice, but everything doesn't have to be by the book."

"Spoken by someone who knows the rules and can break them. It's one thing to commit a social faux pas knowingly and another thing entirely to err from ignorance, the classic example being the poor bumpkin who drinks from his finger bowl at a banquet."

"I guess I do identify with his hostess, who graciously picks up her finger bowl and drinks from it, too," Olivia admitted. "I hope you don't see my attitude as a form of snobbery."

"I see you as a product of your background. A very classy, beautiful product," he added, reaching over to stroke her cheek. His admiring gaze took in her simple skirt and blouse outfit. "I'll bet you get tapped for fashion and beauty advice, too."

It was true, but out of modesty Olivia didn't reply. She was thinking that she didn't exactly like being seen as a "product," a commodity.

"What would you have done if you'd married Eric or Sam?" His question came out of the blue. Evidently he was pursuing his own line of thought. "Would you have continued working? Or quit your job and had time for doing volunteer work? You haven't made any bones about the fact that you're not at heart a career woman," he reminded.

"No, I'm not. I lack the necessary drive and dedication to be a successful career woman. My job is just that, a job that I try to do well, but when I leave the office, I leave the job there." Olivia was repeating things she'd told him in previous conversations.

"So would you have quit after you were married? or was that an option?"

"Yes, it was definitely an option, in both instances."

"Both guys were in pretty high income brackets?"

"Sam is an electrical engineer, and Eric is in management with a big pharmaceutical company. I didn't break off with either one of them because they couldn't support me well," she stated lightly. "Nor did I set my cap for them because they could take care of me in style, if that's what you're thinking. Are you getting nervous that I might have designs on you?"

"My qualms come under a different heading altogether."

"Would you like to explain your qualms? Or can I guess them for myself? Do they all relate to our interwoven past?"

"More or less."

"It's probably wise to steer clear of an open discussion. We might start the weekend off on a low note," Olivia suggested.

"It would be a low note for me if we spoiled the status quo." He reached over and squeezed her hand.

Evidently he was afraid that honesty *would* spoil the status quo. Olivia was afraid of the same thing and, like him, didn't want to take the chance. However tenuous and impermanent their relationship was, she couldn't imagine not seeing Reeves and having him a part of her daily life. Breaking up with him was a thought she couldn't even contemplate at this stage.

"You still haven't answered my question," he said. "Would you have quit your job after you were married?"

"By now I should know to go ahead and answer your questions," she chided him. "If I don't, you'll keep circling back, always the skillful interrogator. Why are you so curious about my engagements to Sam and Eric?"

"Not curious. Interested. I have an intense interest in you."

Olivia sighed. "What woman could resist that tact? Not me, even though I can think of a hundred other topics I'd rather talk about with you than my past love life. Yes, I would have quit my job with the intention of being a full-time wife and mother. Both Sam and Eric wanted a family."

Did Reeves have any desire to be a father? she wondered. It was one of the topics she would rather be talking about.

"I gather you wanted a family, too," he said.

"Yes. Although the idea of being a mother does scare me," Olivia confessed. "Coming from my background, I've had no opportunity to change diapers and baby-sit, like Judy has had, for example."

"You had a nanny," Reeves recalled.

"How do you feel about being a father?"

"I find the idea damned scary, too. My father is a good man, but he wasn't exactly the role model I'd want to be for my son," he pointed out.

"No. Your father will probably make a wonderful grandpa, though, don't you think?"

He nodded after a moment and added, almost glumly, "Providing he ever has a grandchild. The prospects don't look good. I doubt Doreen will have children. And I'm thirty-four."

With obviously no candidate for a wife. Olivia gazed out her window to hide her downcast expression.

"You didn't intend to be a housewife?"

He had resumed his same line of questioning.

Olivia was quick to take offense at his skepticism. "I'm not just decorative. I happen to be quite capable. Judy and I clean our apartment ourselves. Admittedly I'm no Julia Child in the kitchen, but I can cook. I've offered to cook for you," she reminded him. "But you've never taken me up on the offer."

"After you've worked all day at your job, I don't want you cooking for me," he protested soothingly. "It isn't necessary."

"You just can't picture me in a domestic role, can you?"

He shook his head. "It's difficult. I can picture you running a household and creating a lovely home environment. There's where your talents would be utilized, not with mopping floors."

"Lots of housewives in middle America create a lovely home environment *and* mop floors."

"My wife won't have to do housework."

"Lucky her!" Olivia immediately wished that she could take back the sarcastic, jealous rejoinder. It effectively killed the conversation. She sought for a new topic as they rode along in strained silence.

"I like Alan Cramer a lot, by the way. Is he serious about Kay?" she inquired.

Reeves shot her a quick, narrow glance. "Why do you ask?"

She smiled and retorted teasingly, "Isn't it obvious? I brought up his name to get a jealous reaction from you."

"You got one." He smiled back at her and reached for her hand. Olivia laced her fingers with his lean, strong fingers. His hands were as attractive as the rest of him.

She mused, "It struck me the night we played tennis with Alan and Kay that he and Judy might like one another. His dry sense of humor and laid-back manner would appeal to her. I didn't sense any spark between him and Kay."

"He doesn't date anyone else but Kay, but I don't believe he has any marital intentions. If they break off with one another, we'll get him and Judy together. I know he'll think she's cute. Blondes always catch his eye."

"How long has he been involved with Kay?" Olivia asked.

"For about a year and a half."

"That seems like a long time to have a relationship that isn't headed anywhere," she remarked, very casually.

"He likes her a lot, and they have tennis in common. The singles scene gets very old by the time a man gets to be Alan's and my age." He squeezed her hand and returned his to the wheel. "Here's our exit off the interstate onto the scenic route. I'm hoping we can sneak away by ourselves for a walk on the beach about sunset."

Olivia didn't answer, part of her not wanting to drop the topic of lengthy relationships headed nowhere. Did he see their relationship in the same category as Alan and Kay's? she wondered.

"That would be nice to sneak away by ourselves, but I'll be surprised if we can manage it without being antisocial," she said when he looked at her questioningly for some response. "We're not likely to have much private time together this weekend, as I'm sure you realize."

"This is my first experience with being a houseguest for the weekend at someone's summer home," he replied. "I don't know exactly what to expect."

"You can expect marvelous food at every meal, very comfortable accommodations and lots of socializing. I expect that the entire party, William and Debra Sue's houseguests and Marcia and Clinton's, will form one big house party. Marcia and Debra Sue will share the hostessing."

He seemed to be digesting her forecast. "That sounds a little claustrophobic."

"It's enjoyable only if you're with people you like. You definitely wouldn't want to spend that much time in the company of someone who gets on your nerves."

"Is this going to be comfortable for you, being around Duplantis and his wife all weekend? I hadn't realized that we'd be thrown together with them and their guests that much."

"Not terribly comfortable," Olivia admitted honestly.

"Well, why didn't you say as much?" he asked. "I would have turned down the invitation."

"I can handle the situation. If you're going to be a member of William's firm, you'll be socializing with him and Debra Sue."

"William has asked me to give him a definite answer soon," Reeves said soberly. "We had lunch one day this week."

A fact that he hadn't mentioned to her, Olivia reflected. "By now you must have decided."

"I have."

"Are you going to keep me in suspense? I can keep a secret."

"After weighing the pros and cons, I'm going to take the offer."

Why hadn't he told her? Surely he knew that she'd be interested. Olivia felt rebuffed.

"No reaction?" he inquired. "You were a big influence in my decision."

"I was?"

"It matters that I might go up a notch in your estimation. Surely that doesn't surprise you?"

"It pleases me that my opinion carries some weight."

"A great deal of weight."

Olivia's heart lifted. She smiled at him, suddenly feeling on top of the world.

They came to Waveland, Mississippi. The briney sea scent of the Gulf of Mexico was in the air. Riding along in his racy automobile, they drew envious glances.

"This is old hat for you, isn't it?" he remarked. "During the summers you spent whole weeks on the Gulf Coast."

Olivia nodded. "Most of my girlfriends' parents had summer places over here." She smiled at him and accused half-jokingly, "You must have been thrilled to have me gone and out of your hair."

He grinned, but didn't deny it. "I was envious as hell. It seemed like heaven to me to spend whole days on the beach."

"You liked the beach a lot?"

"I liked teenaged girls in bikinis a lot. My hormones were active by then."

"Did you drive over with gangs of friends in high school and have beach parties and picnics?"

"At least several times during the summer."

"You got so suntanned every summer," Olivia recalled, easily conjuring up an image of a teenaged Reeves.

"So did you."

The shared reminiscence wasn't painful or reproachful.

In Bay St. Louis, Reeves braked for a red light, before them the long bridge spanning the bay after which the small town was named. On their right lovely old homes sat on a high bluff. A few miles farther on was their destination, Pass Christian. There, miles of white sand beach began, fronting a succession of picturesque seaside municipalities with marinas serving as home ports for both shrimp boats and yachts. After Pass Christian was Long Beach, then Gulfport, then Biloxi and, lastly, Ocean Springs.

"We'll have to get away by ourselves for a weekend soon," Reeves said with a trace of wistfulness while they were waiting for the traffic light to turn green. "Stay in a motel or rent a condo. A one-bedroom condo," he added. "One of these days I want to sleep with you."

They still hadn't spent the night together at his condo. He hadn't suggested it the night she had come prepared, unbeknownst to him. Needing some encouragement to overcome her qualms, Olivia had gone home.

"We can sleep together this weekend," she assured him. "Nobody will care."

"But you're expecting Marcia to put us in separate bedrooms."

"That's to preserve a sense of decorum. We'll just need to be discreet."

"So I have to sneak into your bedroom." He gave his own translation. "Isn't that preserving a false morality?"

"No, Marcia isn't a prude, but she basically believes in old-fashioned moral behavior. So do I, for that matter," Olivia added. "I'm rather old-fashioned."

"Actually I'm pretty conservative and old-fashioned myself," he admitted. "I don't have any problem with being discreet this weekend."

The light turned to green, and he stepped on the accelerator. The Porsche engine responded, the burst of forward momentum seeming to leave the conversation behind.

Olivia assumed that he meant he believed in marriage and family. No doubt he envisioned himself as having a wife someday who fit his ideal of a life partner and mother of his children.

Did she come even close?

From the long bridge, the view was panoramic, with expanses of placid blue-gray water off to the right and the left as far as the eye could see. Olivia put aside her insecurity and concentrated on appreciating the beauty of the scene.

In Pass Christian, Reeves turned left off Highway 90 onto a street that ran parallel to the busy four-lane highway, but at a higher elevation. Gracious old homes on estate-size lots were set off the quiet street, which was used only for local traffic. Their front porches and balconies commanded a vista of the wide open gulf unobstructed by passing automobiles.

"Here we are. This is Marcia and Clinton's place," Olivia said as they drove abreast of an imposing two-story white house with rambling one-story wings. Tall Corinthian columns supported the roof of a portico at the formal front entrance.

Reeves whistled. "Damn!" he said, braking to a stop. "Their house in the Garden District is modest compared to their summer place."

"It belonged to Clinton's grandmother. She lived here year-round the last forty years or so of her life."

"The place must cost a fortune to maintain," he remarked, shaking his head.

"I'm sure it does, but she also left a fortune to be used for that purpose. She had her lawyers set up a special fund. Otherwise, the place would have been a white elephant and too big a financial burden to keep in the family."

"It must be nice," Reeves mused. "You've been here before?"

"Several times. But never with the husbands along," she added, in case he was wondering whether she'd been invited with a male companion. "I've driven over for the day with Marcia, and one year she had an all-female retreat for our old circle of school friends."

A car horn tooted behind them, and a Mercedes sedan pulled around and passed. It turned into the driveway, entering between stately pillars and proceeding toward the house.

"That was Betty and John Duffy." Olivia identified the couple in the car.

"I met the Duffys at the Hymers' dinner party and we saw them at the reception for Baryshnikov." Reeves sounded anything but enthusiastic, recalling both past occasions.

"Didn't you like them? He's a dear, and she isn't as big a scatterbrain as she might seem."

"They seemed like pleasant people. I liked them fine." He shifted into gear and drove along the street to the entrance.

"Is something wrong?" Olivia ventured, sensing his sudden reluctance. "Are you already having regrets about the weekend?"

"I'm wondering whether Marcia has filled everyone in on me. On who I *am,*" he added.

"By now I'm sure everyone knows the connection. I wouldn't expect the topic to come up in discussion, if that's what's bothering you."

"You would find it damned awkward if the topic did come up in conversation, wouldn't you?"

"I wouldn't be embarrassed," Olivia stated. "But our relationship, past and present, is our personal business."

The Porsche was moving at a crawling pace toward the house.

She went on, urgently wishing to reassure him and yet be open and honest. "The topic that's really sensitive for me is the fact that you and Doreen are brother and sister. I would be embarrassed and ashamed if the subject of the scandal surrounding my grandfather came up in conversation or was even on everyone's minds. But I'm not expecting any awkward moments this weekend." She placed her hand on top of his on the wheel. "Let's don't arrive giving the impression that we're sorry we accepted the invitation. Even if we are."

"Are you sorry?" he asked soberly.

"I had mixed feelings from the very outset."

"Why didn't you say so?"

"Because I didn't want to be a wet blanket. Weekends like this are one of the benefits you'll enjoy as William's partner."

He looked at her closely. "The reason I got the invitation was that I'm dating you."

"No, I was invited because you're dating me. We both were invited because we're dating each other. We're an eligible couple."

The idea of his being in any way responsible for the invitation obviously hadn't occurred to him. It seemed to erase his halfheartedness. He sped up and parked his car behind the Duffys'.

Marcia appeared and ushered them inside. Shortly afterward, Cynthia and Charles Hebert, the third couple staying with the Hymers, arrived. There was jovial confusion as luggage was unloaded and room assignments were made. With all the visiting, it was impossible for Olivia and Reeves to escape to the beach alone, as she had suspected it would be.

That evening Marcia was playing hostess to the Duplantises and their weekend guests. By sunset the whole party had gathered, and cocktails were served outside by the swimming pool. Dinner was New Orleans fare served buffet-style: seafood jambalaya and hot French bread and a mixed green salad. All the talk was of the tennis tournament scheduled to begin the following morning promptly at nine. Amidst much joking and hilarity, the draw was made after the meal, determining who would play whom in the first round of matches.

Reeves had appeared to be enjoying himself up to that point. He became very quiet, Olivia noticed, until the slip of paper with their names written on it was pulled out. After he learned that their opponents were William and Debra Sue Duplantis, he relaxed again, but paid close attention as the poster showing the draw was filled in.

Recalling the practice match against Alan and Kay, Olivia smiled to herself, thinking that the competitive athlete in Reeves had come to the fore. Tomorrow she expected him to be playing to win.

"Are you trying to figure out in advance who our opponents might be in the finals?" She teased him in an undertone.

"Was I that transparent?"

His low reply came readily enough, but sounded slightly forced. "How good are the Duffys?" he asked.

Olivia's gaze went to the poster. Betty and John Duffy were pitted against Sissy and George DeMarco. The team that won out of that match would play her and Reeves, if they emerged victors over the Duplantises.

"They'll probably win over the DeMarcos," she murmured. "Betty is much more athletic than Sissy, and George's main sport is golf."

The expression on Reeves's face said that her prediction was what he was hoping to hear. William Duplantis took that moment to engage them both in conversation, so that Olivia didn't get a chance to probe into Reeves's reasons for preferring to face the Duffys across the tennis net rather than the DeMarcos.

In retrospect he'd had little to say to Sissy and George tonight. The only time he'd left Olivia's side, now that she thought back, was when Sissy came up and began chatting with the two of them. He'd excused himself to go and freshen his drink at the bar.

Had he just been avoiding Sissy?

Olivia had forgotten about running into the DeMarcos and the Bellas at the Theatre of the Performing Arts the evening of the Baryshnikov benefit. Reeves had explained his standoffishness as having to do with his law practice and his handling of medical malpractice lawsuits.

A horrible possibility now flashed into her mind: *Perhaps the doctor in the lawsuit Reeves was currently handling was a physician Sissy and George knew personally.*

But surely not. That doctor must be someone with poor medical credentials, a quack, not a professional acquaintance of George DeMarco's.

An hour later the party broke up. Olivia found herself watching for coolness on Reeves's part toward the DeMarcos. Sure enough, his good-night to them was unmistakably more polite than friendly. Mentally she made a note to question him and air that awful suspicion about the identity of the doctor his client was suing.

His bedroom was across the hall from hers. Changing into a pretty new nightgown, Olivia was filled with bridelike anticipation and bridelike jitters. Troubling conjectures were forgotten.

He eased the door to her bedroom open and came in, wearing slippers and a navy robe over red-and-white-striped pajamas. His whole outfit was obviously new. The pajamas still had creases. The slippers were unscuffed. He looked endearingly sheepish as well as good-looking and virile.

Olivia wore a matching pale pink peignoir over her nightgown. At the sight of her, he whistled softly, an appreciative light gleaming in his dark brown eyes. Smiling with amusement and unexpectedly shy, she went up close to him and fussed with the lapels of his robe.

"Did you go out and buy new pajamas?" she asked.

"No. I have a whole drawerful that my mother has given me for presents," he replied. "She gave me the robe and the slippers, too."

"You don't sleep in pajamas."

"I sleep in my underwear." He fingered the lace of her peignoir. "Is your outfit new?"

"Brand-new. Do you like it?"

"I like you in it," he said with soft fervor. "Although *like* is not quite the word."

Her heart gave a leap at his tone and his expression. She held her breath, expecting his next words to be, *I love you in it.* But he took her into his arms and kissed her, leaving the sentiment unspoken.

For just a second, disappointment kept her from responding. The time had seemed so right to verbalize deep emotions. If he had spoken his words, Olivia could have spoken hers. *I love you in any kind of clothes.*

Because she didn't just adore Reeves...she *loved* him. And he loved her.

The denial of expression made the mutual caring disturbingly, frighteningly intense. Their lovemaking was almost unbearably tender, bringing a sweet, aching satisfaction. Olivia lay silent in his arms afterward, happiness warring with fear.

"What? No conversation?" he inquired, possessiveness and ardor in his voice.

"I guess we've switched roles," she murmured. "Tonight I'm struck mute. Or that's not true. I just don't dare open my mouth for fear of what might come out."

"What might come out?" he urged softly. "The same words that have been choking me for weeks? Why do you think I don't dare talk after we make love?"

Olivia braced herself against the thrill shooting through her. "Who's going to go first?"

"I will. I love you."

She planted a kiss on his bare chest and felt a hard tremor run through him. "I love you."

He hugged her so tightly she couldn't breathe, but his strength only increased her sense of vulnerability.

"Love isn't an altogether good feeling, is it?" she said. "In reality it doesn't take away the element of uncertainty like it does in movies and books."

"It may not be an altogether good feeling," Reeves concurred, kissing her hair, "but I wouldn't change places with any other man in the universe right this second."

"I wouldn't change places with any other woman."

"Now let's say good-night and go to sleep, sweetheart. Tomorrow we have a tennis tournament to play."

"I hope I won't be a liability," she worried, but her sigh arose out of a deeper worry entirely.

"You won't be. You couldn't possibly be a liability to me. Just by being on the court, you'll inspire me to show off and impress you."

They told each other good-night and spoke the newly minted words of love again. Olivia wondered in her heart if she could also utter a simple variation of *I love you*, substituting *trust* for *love*.

Chapter Eleven

The next day, Olivia remembered her intention to question Reeves about his lack of friendliness toward Sissy and George, but it wasn't a pressing concern and didn't weigh on her mind. There was little opportunity for such a discussion since the two of them had limited time alone together.

Most of their private conversation consisted of quick exchanges. A great deal of thrilling unspoken communication transpired with frequent touching and smiles and loving, admiring glances.

Olivia could feel her happiness growing into bliss, crowding out her fear of being in love with him. All the problems facing them seemed easily surmountable, including the fact that Doreen was his sister. Last night's lack of trust seemed exaggerated out of all proportion.

Thanks to his athleticism and superior ability as a tennis player, they easily won their matches on Saturday and were in the finals scheduled for Sunday morning. Olivia improved with each match, as her timing got better. Playing tennis had been a part of her social background. She'd been taught proper form and was reasonably well coordinated. Reeves's competitiveness was contagious. She found herself wanting to win because she was his partner. Every point earned was a mutual accomplishment, a point for *them*.

For all his aggressiveness, he was sportsmanlike and a gentleman on the court. He eased up on his serve to the women and saved his powerful serves and wicked overheads and volleys for the men. Olivia's pride in him grew. She basked in the compliments and read the subtle language that said Reeves met with the approval of these people in her former world.

He could gain broader acceptance into that world, evidently a goal for him. It was possible for him to become socially prominent himself, as he would apparently like to be, the condition being that when he married, he would need to marry a woman who was acceptable, a woman who would be an asset, not a liability.

Olivia had the qualifications, despite her misfortunes. She had the background, the social know-how, the right contacts. The question was whether she could fit herself into the mold of a Marcia and Debra Sue, dedicate herself to being a society wife.

She hadn't expected ever to have anything but her past in common with Marcia and Sissy and Betty Duffy and Debra Sue Duplantis. Now suddenly it was conceivable that her life could be similar to theirs if she married Reeves.

The idea took some mental adjustment. It would be a big transition for her, returning from another kind of life entirely. Olivia was a changed person now, a different person than she would have become if she hadn't suffered misfortune. She had a whole different kind of pride.

But the thought of being Reeves's wife and making him happy was a totally joyful thought. Olivia reminded herself not to start planning the wedding, though, until he'd proposed to her. There was no assurance that his mind was running on the same track as hers.

William and Debra Sue Duplantis were host and hostess for cocktails and dinner Saturday night. Late in the afternoon Olivia and Reeves went inside to shower and change. He was quiet and seemed preoccupied with his own thoughts.

Outside the door to Olivia's room, he commented rather wistfully, "I don't suppose we could pass up the cocktail hour and take a walk down to the beach instead."

"Not without being rude."

He nodded, looking resigned.

"We can say our goodbyes after lunch tomorrow and stop off at the beach on our way back to New Orleans," she said consolingly, wanting to cheer him up. "Or maybe we can call it an early evening and squeeze in a moonlight walk down to the beach."

"Let's do that," he urged, but the plan didn't visibly brighten his sober mood, making her wonder if something else wasn't bothering him. There was no opportunity to ask because Charles and Cynthia Hebert were headed up the stairs, on the way to their rooms down the same hallway.

The moonlight walk was doomed from the outset of the evening not to happen. Debra Sue served delicious hors d'oeuvres with cocktails, and dinner ended up being rather late. After dinner, the Hymers and their houseguests all left together, trooping the distance between the two summer houses on foot. Unused to as much physical exertion as she'd had that day, Olivia was too tired to want to walk to the beach. Reeves didn't even suggest it.

Stifling yawns, the four couples said good-night on their arrival. In her room Olivia donned her nightgown and peignoir. When Reeves didn't slip over from his room after a few minutes had passed, she decided to go over and find out what was delaying him.

He hadn't even begun to get undressed, but sat sprawled in an armchair, sunk deeply in thought.

"Is something wrong?" Olivia asked worriedly, quietly closing the door behind her. "Are you upset with me?"

"No, I'm not upset with you," he denied readily. "Why should I be?" He stood up slowly. "Just give me a couple of minutes."

She smiled, and cajoled, "Can I stay and watch you put on your pajamas?"

"Sure. In fact, we can sleep in here. Then I won't have to put on my pajamas." He moved over to the queen-size bed and turned back the covers for her.

Assured of her welcome, Olivia removed her peignoir and got into the bed while he removed his shirt and slacks. He went into the adjoining bathroom briefly and then returned and climbed in next to her, wearing his dark briefs. She sat with a pillow behind her back and didn't need any urging to scoot close to him into the strong circle of his arm.

"Alone at last," she said with a soulful sigh. Although bone weary, she wasn't sleepy, she felt like talking. Maybe he would share with her whatever was bothering him. "Today was loads of fun. I've never enjoyed tennis so much."

"It was fun," he agreed. "And I could tell that you were enjoying yourself today." He tightened his arm, giving her a hug.

"You're really marvelous."

"Thanks. I love the game."

"Everyone was impressed with your playing. Tonight I overheard John Duffy offering to sponsor you if you were interested in joining the New Orleans Country Club. His sponsorship practically guarantees that you would be approved as a member, you know," she added.

"You must have heard me tell him that I was interested," he replied quietly.

"I did," Olivia replied.

"He'd had a couple of martinis. I wouldn't hold him to his offer." Before she could answer, he remarked, "Your grandparents would turn over in their graves. They were members of New Orleans Country Club, weren't they?"

"Yes, they were." And he was right. They would turn over in their graves, Olivia reflected.

"William has offered to sponsor me if I want to join New Orleans Lawn Tennis. Of course, I'm sure his offer is conditional."

"He'll make good on it once you're a member of the Duplantis law firm."

"Right."

"William is quite a fan of yours in the courtroom as well as on the tennis court. He cornered me before dinner to tell me what a brilliant attorney you are and to enlist me as his ally in persuading you to join Duplantis & Duplantis." Olivia's pride in Reeves was in her voice.

"I saw you talking to him. So did Debra Sue."

"Neither one of you has any cause for jealousy. There isn't so much as a spark between William and me. He feels guilty about me, I suspect, and probably senses that I have no admiration or respect for him as a man."

"Confidentially, I don't have a very high regard for William as an attorney. Alan Cramer has a much sharper legal mind. So do the other attorneys in my office building."

Olivia waited, thinking that he meant to add something. When he didn't, she followed up on his remarks. "Surely Duplantis & Duplantis has some sharp attorneys."

"Of course it does." He sighed.

Olivia kissed him on the cheek. "Well, it's my unbiased opinion that you'll soon be Duplantis & Duplantis's star attorney."

"You're completely in favor of my making the career change, aren't you?"

"Everything seems to point in the direction of its being a good move for you. Are you having second thoughts?"

"Not really." But he sighed again as he hugged her tightly.

Olivia rubbed cheeks with him. "Let's talk about something else." She cast around in her mind for a different subject and remembered his coolness toward the DeMarcos. "There's something that I've been wanting to ask you about. Why are you so uncomfortable around the DeMarcos? Does it have something to do with your medical malpractice case?"

His arm around her shoulders tensed to hard steel. "Yes, it does," he affirmed finally.

"I was afraid of that," she said regretfully. "Please tell me that the doctor being sued isn't a well-known physician who might be a friend of theirs." Her heart sank when he didn't answer. Some ghastly intuition had made her guess the truth. "Reeves, you can't really be bringing a lawsuit against a reputable doctor who isn't a quack!"

"I'm turning the case over to another attorney," he said gravely. "But purely because of the conflict of interest. The weight of evidence against the doctor clearly indicates malpractice."

"I'll take your word for it." Olivia didn't want to get into a discussion of the case. She didn't want to be at odds with him over anything. "I'm just glad that you're going to let some other lawyer handle the lawsuit. Did you decide to do that this weekend?"

"No, weeks ago."

Then why had he felt so awkward around Sissy and George? They wouldn't necessarily have to know that he'd ever had any connection to the lawsuit.

"Have you been unable to find another attorney?"

"No, there's a good woman attorney who handles medical malpractice cases. I haven't approached her yet, but I'm confident she'll gladly take on my client. I've taken all the depositions and done the legal groundwork," he explained.

Olivia could hear the reluctance in his voice. Obviously he wasn't especially happy about handing over the case, perhaps because of a big sum of money involved.

"I'm sure it will work out for the best," she soothed. "In the long run you'll be glad."

"I hope so," he said. "I'm meeting with my client on Monday."

"Good. Then you can make friends with the De-Marcos with a clear conscience." She slipped her arms around him and hugged him. "Now let's forget about your law practice for a while and carry on some pillow talk, shall we? I'll start. I love you, Mr. Attorney and ace tennis player."

"I love you," he said softly, reaching to snap off the lamp and plunge the room into darkness.

They slid lower in the bed. Olivia nestled closely in his arms, happiness welling up in her.

"I felt so *happy* today," she confided. "Happier than I've been in years."

"I want to make you happy, Olivia."

She wished that he *sounded* happier himself.

"I could easily get in the habit of sleeping in the same bed with you," she said drowsily. "Here we are like two tired old married people, me in my nightgown and you in your underwear." His hand stroked downward along her back, arousing delicate pleasure. "Did I ever tell you what wonderful, talented hands you have?"

"Some things bear repeating," he suggested, his tone deep and intimate. And *loving,* like the touch of his hand.

Olivia's drowsiness and fatigue were vanishing. She put her hand to work, discovering him hard and aroused. "You're in no condition to go to sleep," she observed.

He was caressing her bare skin beneath the night-gown. His hand slid between her thighs. She sucked in her breath as he explored with sensitive fingertips and commented on his findings, murmuring, "You're in no condition to go to sleep, either."

"I love having you touch me there," she whispered, and moaned as he set off spasms of delicious sensation with his gentle rubbing and probing.

"I love touching you here . . . and everywhere."

He groaned with his own intense pleasure as she fondled him intimately and made explicit, appreciative comments. They carried on a graphic lovers' dialogue as they made love, but it was a dialogue full of the nuance of deep caring.

Nothing could compare with the ecstatic joy that Olivia experienced when Reeves entered her with the words, "I love you, Olivia."

Her climax was only a bonus.

Reeves had never been a real believer in the power of love before, but he was a believer now. Popular romantic-comedy metaphors had applied to him before. He'd been "caught, hook, line and sinker." He'd fallen "head over heels." He'd been "at the beck and call" of a few females for a limited period of time.

This was different. It was serious. It was alarming. Olivia *mattered* so much to him. She had become *necessary* in his life. For the first time, Reeves understood how a man could be swayed by a woman to betray a higher purpose, to compromise ideals, to change his inner self.

For Olivia to be in love with him was like a miracle he didn't dare buy until it proved to be real and lasting. He couldn't quite accept that she loved *him,* the man he was. But Reeves wanted like hell to be the man she could love, the man she would want to marry.

If necessary, he would model himself after William Duplantis, for, deep down, Reeves was convinced that Duplantis represented Olivia's ideal husband—successful, polished, civic-minded, highly respectable. The more Reeves was like Duplantis and the less he was like her ex-fiancés, Eric and Sam, the better his chance of putting his ring on her finger for keeps.

He liked the Hymers and the Duffys and even the DeMarcos well enough. In time he might find them more interesting as people. Perhaps some sense of real rapport might develop. Eventually he would start to feel more at ease around them and not have to be on his best polite behavior. The socializing would probably become genuine visiting and not seem so banal and superficial.

What was important was for Olivia to be happy and fulfilled. Reeves could adapt for her sake. This weekend was proof beyond a doubt that she still belonged in her old society world, not out in Metairie. It did Reeves's heart good to watch her. Her smile, her voice, her laugh, her whole manner said that she was happily in her element.

As *his* wife, she could return to uptown New Orleans and hold her head up high. She could hostess luncheons, chair fund-raising committees, and come into her own again. That was the unbelievable—and edifying—irony in the whole situation.

It was a heady thought for Reeves that *he*, Reeves Talbot, could give Olivia all that. In return, he could have her for a lifetime companion. No sacrifice seemed too great.

By Sunday, Reeves had come to the realization that there was no turning back for him. He had bought into the whole program this weekend: he would definitely join Duplantis & Duplantis and tailor himself into Olivia's husband.

He served the final point of the match. A clean ace. To the sound of enthusiastic applause from the onlookers, Olivia tossed her racket down and whirled around, both arms in the air. Slim and sexy and lovely in her white tennis outfit, she ran to him at the baseline, threw her arms around his neck and kissed him in front of everyone.

"We won! We're the champions!" she exclaimed as he hugged her tight, lifting her off the ground.

She's mine! Reeves was exulting in his heart. *I've won her!*

A mock-serious ceremony followed, declaring them the winners. They posed for snapshots, holding an ornate silver chalice on which their names would be engraved, in the tradition of Wimbledon.

"This means you have to come back next year and defend your title," a chorus of voices informed them.

Several of the women added the confident prediction, "They won't be the team of Prescott and Talbot next year. They'll be the Talbots. Anyone want to take bets on that?"

The response was loudly and good-naturedly unanimous, no takers on the bet.

Blushing, Olivia met Reeves's gaze. Her beauty took his breath away. Her black hair formed a glorious halo of waves and curls, framing her face. Her eyes were that incredibly lovely shade of violet-blue. Pink color tinged her creamy, flawless complexion. She was radiant with happiness. She glowed with pride and adoration.

Pride *in him.* Adoration *for him.* Reeves smiled at her, not caring that the message must be written plain on his face that he felt the most fortunate of men to have her look at him with that expression.

In that public moment, any small doubt was erased.
Olivia would marry him. He could say casually right
now, "How about it?" and she would accept his proposal in the same light vein. Later he could propose
again, speaking the traditional question, "Will you
marry me?" Her answer would be thrillingly simple.
"Yes. I will."

Reeves almost gave in to the urge, but something held
him back. Instead, he kissed her lightly on the mouth,
making a nonverbal kind of assent to the assumption
that they would be man and wife next year.

"Between now and next year's tournament, Olivia
and I will have time to practice our mixed doubles," he
warned.

Immediately there was discussion about making dates
for playing mixed doubles in the coming months. The
spotlight of attention was off the two of them. Olivia
gave no outward sign that he had disappointed her, but
Reeves sensed that he had.

The walk on the beach didn't materialize that afternoon, either. The sun still shone brightly when they left
the Hymers' summer home about midafternoon. They
agreed to content themselves with a drive along the
beach route to Ocean Springs before heading back home
to New Orleans.

"I'm sorry we didn't get to the beach," Olivia said
without any serious regret. "Next time."

"Next time," Reeves agreed.

She gazed out her window, musing, "This turned out
to be a marvelous weekend. I'm glad you decided to accept for us. The company was good and the food delicious. We had perfect weather and lots of exercise." She
smiled over at him. "And, the icing on the cake—you
for my roommate."

"I was about to get my nose out of joint," he teased, making an effort to match his mood to hers.

"You seemed to enjoy yourself as much as I did."

Her statement called for some reassurance.

"I did enjoy myself. Marcia and Clinton are an outstanding hostess and host. The group couldn't have been more congenial. It was a very pleasant weekend." Reeves reached over and squeezed her hand. "I was able to be with you. That was the best part."

"Everyone likes you very much."

"They liked the side of my personality that I showed them anyway," he replied. "We all used good manners."

"Being courteous comes so naturally to you. And you hold your own in any conversation." Amusement rippled in her voice. "You even managed to look interested and reply intelligently when Betty Duffy got off on the subject of her children."

"I was put to the test in that conversation," Reeves admitted. "Being an effective courtroom attorney involves some acting. I was trying to make a good impression this weekend. You do realize that? I wasn't in my natural element, like you were. I felt under a strain."

"It certainly didn't show."

He couldn't let the matter drop. Some honest compulsion made him go on and expose his insecurity. "I was nervous on the way over here. Couldn't you tell? This was my first tennis tournament played on private courts in the backyards of summer homes that come damned close to being mansions."

"You would get used to it. Marcia and Clinton will probably invite us again before the summer is over, the next time for a sailing weekend. They keep their sailboat over here during the summer."

"Let me guess. There's an annual private regatta, too."

Olivia laughed. "Not to my knowledge, but if there were, our crew would win. I'm sure you're a wonderful sailor, too."

"I've only been sailing a couple of times."

"As a novice you would still be a wonderful sailor." She sighed contentedly and changed the subject, commenting on the swimsuit fashions of a group of teenagers engaged in a game of volleyball on the white-sand beach.

Reeves didn't get the chance to air his gut reaction to spending another social weekend with the Hymers and their inner circle of friends in the near future. The thought was stifling. He hoped the invitation didn't materialize for several months.

When they could manage to get away for another long weekend, he wanted to spend it with Olivia, not in the company of a group and certainly not the same group. If he were picking companions, he would prefer another couple who weren't married and settled. Alan and Kay, for example.

"I feel ridiculously happy," Olivia mused. "It's all because of *us.*"

Reeves knew that her happiness didn't stem solely from their relationship. It was the total picture filling her with optimism for the future. He was only a component in that picture, but better to be a component than not to figure in the picture.

He could win where her luckless ex-fiancés had lost out.

His family ties with his parents and his sister needn't pose an insurmountable problem. Reeves could keep his family relationships separate from his marriage. There was nothing to keep him from talking to his parents as often on the telephone as he did now. He could visit them in Florida once or twice a year, with or without her.

As for his sister, the truth was that the two of them had little in common other than being brother and sister. No matter whom Reeves married, he wasn't likely to be inviting Doreen to his home on a regular basis. It went against his grain not to be able to invite her to his home at all, but he could live with the situation in order to share a home with Olivia.

Reeves could meet Doreen for lunch and talk to her on the phone as often as he did now, which wasn't very often. The two of them might plan a trip to Florida occasionally for a family get-together.

Would that things might have been different, of course, but he had never thought in terms of a future wife marrying into his family. His wife would be marrying *him,* and he would be marrying *her,* not her family. Married life would include family on both sides, he'd assumed, but not to any great extent. Reeves had never welcomed the idea of intrusive relatives.

Olivia didn't have any family. He wouldn't be plagued with troublesome in-laws. That was the other side of the coin.

On the drive to New Orleans, Reeves's mind worked on two tracks. He kept up his end of the conversation and concentrated on the present while he looked ahead into the future and found pragmatic solutions to problems.

It occurred to him that the problems should be *their* problems, not just *his.* He should be bringing up concerns openly, not trying to solve them in advance on his own. Marriage was a partnership, with concessions and accommodations on both sides.

At least that had been his definition.

He took Olivia directly to her apartment in Metairie. After carrying her luggage inside and exchanging a few pleasantries with Judy, he resisted the temptation to stay longer. The next day he expected to be finishing up a case in court and needed to work on his summation, among other things.

"You mean those great speeches that lawyers make to juries aren't ad-lib?" Judy demanded. "How disillusioning!"

"Judy is a great fan of TV shows and movies with courtroom trials," Olivia put in.

Her apartment mate addressed him earnestly, "Tell me truthfully, Reeves. Do any of you lawyers really care about justice being served? Or is it just a matter of winning a case and earning a fee, the bigger the better?"

"There are quite a few of us who care," he replied in the same serious vein. "I do, and I can personally vouch for some other attorneys with whom I'm associated. One of them Olivia has met. Alan Cramer."

"Reeves and I plan to get you and Alan together when he breaks off with his current girlfriend." Olivia spoke up gaily.

There was no intention on her part, he knew, to cut off his answer, but he felt frustrated. His words had really been for her benefit, not Judy's. He wanted her to hear him state his policy of accepting clients he wished to represent and turning away others whose cases might involve larger fees or fees just as large.

As an attorney with Duplantis & Duplasntis, he wouldn't have that freedom.

Olivia saw him to the door, where she hugged him and kissed him and told him goodbye with a reluctance that partially soothed a deep-seated dissatisfaction.

"I already miss you," she said softly. "Will you call me later before I go to bed and say good-night?"

Reeves promised, having no premonition that it might be a promise he would break.

He drove to his office. From there he rang his number at his condo to check the messages on his answering machine. One of the messages was from Rachel Wade. It made him swear violently with compassion and revived all his outrage on Bill Wade's behalf.

Bill Wade had shot himself that morning in a suicide attempt. He was hospitalized and in critical condition.

There was no aid that Reeves could render at the hospital, but the despair and hopelessness in Rachel Wade's voice tore at his guts. He felt a human obligation to go and express his sympathy to her and try to bolster her courage. If he could help out in some practical way, he would determine how.

She sat in a waiting room. With her were the two older Wade children and several other family members. They all seemed to take heart at his presence.

"It was so good of you to come, Mr. Talbot," Mrs. Wade repeated several times.

"What if my dad d-dies?" her teenaged son blurted out to Reeves. He swallowed hard and ducked his head, struggling not to break down. "Does that mean that doctor can't be sued for messing up my dad's operation?"

"No, it doesn't mean that, Billy," Reeves assured the boy grimly. "It doesn't mean that at all."

"Good. Because this is his fault. He put my dad in this fix. I wish somebody would *kill*—" His voice broke. "Kill him."

"Billy! You don't wish that!" his mother admonished sadly.

"Yes, I do wish it. Then he couldn't operate on somebody else."

Reeves ached with empathy for the boy, who, thanks to Dr. Bella, would never toss a football to his dad again or wrestle with him on the living room carpet.

Do any of you lawyers really care about justice being served? Judy Hays's question rang clear in his mind. Reeves's answer rang clear, too. *I do.*

Leaving the hospital, Reeves knew that he wasn't going to pass Bill Wade's case on to another attorney. It simply *wasn't* the right thing for him to do, as an attorney, as a man.

All along he'd known that.

All along he'd known deep down that being an attorney with Duplantis & Duplantis wasn't for him.

Could Olivia possibly understand? It was hoping for a miracle, but he had to hope that she really did love *him.*

Tomorrow night Reeves would know. He would tell her everything, about the Bill Wade case involving a lawsuit against Dr. Bella, about his intention to turn down the offer from Duplantis & Duplantis, about his doubts and insecurities regarding her.

Tonight he wouldn't call her.

He didn't trust himself to sound normal and not give away that something was wrong.

Chapter Twelve

"Don't hold out on me! Did you get a marriage proposal from Reeves this weekend?" Judy demanded eagerly when Olivia came back into the living room.

"No, he didn't ask me to marry him. But he loves me. And I love him. I *really* love him, Judy." Olivia sighed happily, sinking into an armchair and drawing up her legs in preparation for a heart-to-heart talk. "This is really *it*. It's true that you *know* when the right man comes along."

"Haven't I been telling you that! Olivia, I'm so happy for you that I've got chill bumps." She shivered and rubbed her arms. "Describe for me in detail how you *know* that you and Reeves are meant for each other."

"We admire each other. I almost burst with pride when I'm around him, not just because he's so attractive. He has such fine qualities. I haven't discovered a single flaw in his character or personality. And he seems to think I'm perfect exactly the way I am. He makes me feel good about myself."

"Is that different from your past serious relationships? Didn't they make you feel good about yourself?"

"Yes, but not to the same extent. I wasn't *right* for them the way I am for Reeves. I can be the perfect wife for him, be the wife he wants and needs, to make him happy."

"Is he the perfect husband for you? Do you want the same things in life?"

"I can make his goals my own. I'll get enormous satisfaction out of being his marriage partner. My self-esteem won't suffer at all if my main recognition comes from the title, Mrs. Reeves Talbot." Olivia's voice was dreamy and yet certain.

"You and Reeves will live in uptown New Orleans?"

"My guess is that he'll want a home in the Garden District. We'll probably entertain a lot, have a busy social life. But we'll have an ordinary family life, too. I'll see to that. I'll make sure our children grow up in a secure home and are taught real values. They won't be little snobs." She hugged herself, entranced with the vision. "If he doesn't propose soon, Judy, I'm not sure I can be patient. I may ask *him* to marry me!"

"No, don't do that," Judy advised. "Let Reeves propose. I'll bet he's planning to make a romantic occasion out of it. Candlelight, roses, champagne, you in a beautiful gown and him in a tux or a dinner jacket." She sighed rapturously. "Will you have a big wedding? You and Reeves will make a bride and groom right out of a picture book..." Her voice drifted off and her expression grew concerned. "Oh, dear. What about his sister? I forgot all about her."

Olivia had put Doreen out of her mind, too. She shrugged. "There's no changing the fact that she's his sister. I won't let her be a dividing factor between us."

"Does Reeves know that's your outlook? Maybe you should tell him. He may be thinking that his family is an obstacle."

"I've commented more than once to him about how fond I was of his parents in years past."

"Yes, but they were your servants at the time. You said just now that Reeves doesn't have any character flaws. Remember you accused him early in your relationship of having a chip on his shoulder. Did it disappear? Or could he be covering up some feelings of inferiority?"

"Reeves with an inferiority complex!" Olivia scoffed. "That's hard for me to imagine. He's impressed by wealth, but he radiates a healthy self-confidence."

"I agree that it's hard to imagine that he could have a confidence problem," Judy conceded. "Back to Doreen, won't you be forced to invite her to the wedding?"

Olivia nodded. "Yes, I'll have to invite her. But I doubt she'll come. She hates me more than I hate her. After the run-in with her in the French Quarter, I almost feel sorry for Doreen. Reeves helped me that day to see things better from her point of view."

"Is he aware that your feelings about her have softened?"

"I guess not. We don't ever discuss Doreen. Since he hasn't proposed, there's been no opportunity to say that I wouldn't exclude his sister from our wedding."

"He'll propose soon," Judy predicted.

Olivia bit her lip, slightly worried now. "There's more than my attitude to consider. I've never even asked him whether he's mentioned to his parents that he's dating me. What if they don't approve? They may remember me as a spoiled brat."

"I'll bet they'll be delighted to have you for a daughter-in-law. Now, I'm dying to hear about your weekend. What kind of meals were you served? Were there servants waiting on you hand and foot? Describe the houses for me...."

She pressed Olivia for details, and Olivia obligingly provided them, satisfying Judy's curiosity about a lifestyle that she found endlessly fascinating.

Later that night when she was getting ready for bed, Olivia found herself wondering, *Would the weekend have been any less enjoyable had everything been on a more modest scale? What if the houses hadn't been so large and luxurious? What if the food had been hot dogs and hamburgers cooked on the grill and the beverages had been canned colas and beer and jug wine?*

It wouldn't have been the *same* weekend. But it could have been fun in a different way, even with different people, as long as they were people she and Reeves both liked.

The only thing that couldn't be changed was having him there. His presence had made the weekend delightful. Without him, the company of old friends in comfortable surroundings and excellent food and drink and the fun of participating in the tennis tournament wouldn't have added up to happiness and contentment.

When he'd call tonight—and she was expecting the phone to ring any second—she would tell him that, in case he hadn't figured it out for himself.

Olivia settled herself in bed with a magazine. Soon she was fighting drowsiness. By eleven-thirty she had dozed off several times and awakened to blink at the light shed by her lamp.

Reeves must have let the time get past him and then not wanted to call and take the chance of waking her and Judy. After some groggy deliberation, Olivia decided against calling him and possibly waking him out of a sound sleep. He probably had this same feeling of pleasant fatigue that comes with vigorous exercise.

Good-night, my darling. Sleep well. Turning off the lamp, she sent the thought to him and curled up on her side, warmed by her love and secure in the confidence that he hadn't deliberately broken his promise to call her tonight.

She had absolute trust in Reeves....

"Olivia, this is Sissy."

Olivia's first reaction was disappointment. All morning she'd been expecting Reeves to call her at work, but so far he hadn't. The sense of letdown immediately faded with the realization that Sissy was upset about something.

"Hi, Sissy. Is something wrong? I can always tell by your voice."

"Something's very wrong, but I'd rather not talk about it on the phone. Could you please have lunch with me today?"

"Well, of course, I can." Olivia noted the time. It was eleven-fifteen. "But put my mind at ease, won't you? You and George and the children are all right? There's no serious health problem."

"None of us has been diagnosed with any incurable disease." The assurance was uncharacteristically bitter. "Not any new one, anyway. The crisis that's come up concerns my father, Olivia."

"Dr. Bella?"

"I'll explain at lunch."

After she'd hung up, Olivia called Reeves's office, not really expecting him to be there. She assumed that he was probably in court and hadn't been able to get to a phone. Otherwise surely he would have called by now to apologize for breaking his promise last night and not calling to say good-night.

His secretary, Joan, confirmed that he indeed was in court and would be tied up all day. She mentioned the name of the judge.

Resuming her interrupted task, Olivia reflected with a rush of pride that she wanted to see Reeves in action in a courtroom. One day soon she would arrange to take off from work when he had a trial scheduled.

Thoughts of Sissy occupied her mind during the next forty-five minutes. What "crisis" had come up involving Dr. Bella? Sissy's cryptic, bitter remark about no *new* health problem had been diagnosed, added to the enigma.

Was there an old health problem? Was Dr. Bella an alcoholic? To her dismay, Olivia didn't find the possibility unlikely. When had she ever seen him without a drink in his hand?

The fact that Sissy was coming to her with the problem bore out the intuition. Among Sissy's close friends, who better than Olivia could empathize with a crisis involving shame and embarrassment and loss of respect for a revered father figure.

At Sissy's suggestion, they'd agreed to have a lunch of take-out Chinese food at Olivia's apartment. Pale and visibly distraught, Sissy got out of her BMW when Olivia drove into the parking lot.

The two women hugged each other, not a polite hug of greeting, but a supportive embrace on Olivia's part.

"You can't imagine how horrible this all is," Sissy said, then contradicted herself. "Yes, you can, after all you went through with your grandfather."

Inside the apartment, Olivia led the way to the kitchen. Sissy sat down at the table in the dining alcove. Without any preamble, she announced in a tone of utter despair, "My father's an alcoholic, as you may or may not have suspected. He's botched up an operation. He's going to be sued for malpractice."

"Sued for malpractice?" Olivia repeated in appalled disbelief. "Dr. Bella?" Numbly she sat down at the table, lunch forgotten.

"It will go before the medical review board. His insurance company will pay a huge settlement out of court, but the news will get out. Everyone will know. Oh, God, Olivia, my poor mother! She won't be able to hold up her head. And my father will drink himself to death, trying to drown his guilt over ruining that man's life. The whole thing is just a nightmare." Sissy buried her face in her hands. "I wish I could wake up and find that it was all a bad dream."

"I know that feeling," Olivia said in a comforting tone, aching with empathy. She wished she could say, *Everything will be all right,* but everything wouldn't be all right. Her mind searched for some avenue of hope. "Can the operation be done again and the damage corrected?"

Sissy shook her head slowly. Her words were muffled by her hands. "No, there were severed nerves."

"Can't that sort of thing easily happen during delicate surgery? Maybe it isn't a clear case of your father's being at fault."

"It is a clear case." Sissy raised her head, revealing a bleak, ravaged face. "The only hope is to stop the lawsuit now before the matter goes before the state review board. Then the public scandal might be avoided. I was hoping that Reeves might help."

"Of course," Olivia murmured, suddenly chilled to the marrow. *Dear God, the medical malpractice lawsuit Reeves had been handling wasn't against Dr. Bella, was it? No, of course, it wasn't.*

A sickening dread slowly spread through her.

The pieces all fit, starting with his behavior on their first date when they'd encountered Dr. and Mrs. Bella and George and Sissy. His discomfort around Sissy and George this weekend suddenly made horrible sense as did his unwillingness to discuss the lawsuit with Olivia.

Please, God, don't let it be true. The thought was unbearable that the whole time Olivia had been falling in love with Reeves and learning to trust him, he might have been proceeding with a damaging lawsuit against the father of one of her oldest friends. Worst of all, he would have been carefully concealing the fact from her.

"Would you talk to Reeves, explain everything and get his reaction?" Sissy asked. "He hasn't seemed to warm to me or I would go to him myself."

"I'll be seeing him tonight," Olivia said numbly. "I'll find out then."

No, she couldn't wait until tonight. She would call in sick this afternoon and go downtown to the courthouse. There wouldn't be any point in returning to her job anyway. How could she function with the love in her heart turning to doubt?

All the pieces fit, but maybe—*maybe*—they didn't really fit. Olivia had to find out without any delay that

Reeves wasn't cut out of the same cloth as her grandfather.

Court was in session. Olivia took a seat just inside the door, remembering her wish earlier that day to see Reeves in action. He sat at a table next to a woman who was presumably his client. She had tinted red hair and was poorly dressed, Olivia could see at a glance. Both her black suit jacket and shocking-pink blouse were polyester. The jacket was poorly tailored, the seams at the shoulders puckered.

In marked contrast, Reeves's dark brown jacket was expensive, fitting his broad shoulders as though custom-tailored. Olivia felt a little thrill of pride, some of her terrible doubt subsiding. *Her suspicions were silly. Reeves was honest and dependable as a rock. She just knew he was.*

At another table were two attorneys with briefcases open in front of them. They were obviously part of a high-powered team. Their third member was on his feet addressing a jury.

The judge reared back in his tall chair behind the bench with a bored expression on his jowled face.

This was Reeves's world of law now. The woman was the type of client he represented as a plaintiff lawyer. Once he'd joined Duplantis & Duplantis, that would change. He would represent a different class of client, Olivia reflected, concentrating on the proceedings.

The spokesman for the team of attorneys sat down, and Reeves rose to his feet to present his summation. Approaching the jury, he outlined the case as though the six people were hearing the facts for the first time. His client's name was May Pickens. She was suing a major discount department store chain for injury sustained on the premises of one of its stores. She had been shopping in the store, he explained matter-of-factly, when a whole section of shelving with merchandise collapsed on top of her. She'd suffered broken ribs and a broken hip. A sharp object had struck her in the left eye, resulting in the complete loss of vision in that eye.

Her disabilities had made it impossible for her to hold down her waitress's job, which provided the sole income for herself and two children. Her car had been repossessed. She'd had to go on welfare. She and her children had suffered the indignities of poverty as well the financial hardships.

Reeves went on to summarize the testimony of various witnesses establishing that the discount store was liable. He was asking the jury to award monetary compensation for past and future unearned income and for physical and psychological pain and suffering.

Noting how even the judge had grown alert, Olivia glowed with pride. Now she could fully appreciate why William wanted Reeves in the family firm enough to overlook his background. Reeves *would* be Duplantis & Duplantis's star attorney. May Pickens deserved compensation. She'd been a victim.

Coming here today had been very enlightening. Olivia had gained a whole new insight into Reeves's law practice that only made her admire him more. Yesterday he'd declared to Judy that he cared about justice. Olivia hadn't doubted his words, but she hadn't appreciated his sincerity as she did now. He *did* care about justice. His law practice was about more than drumming up cases and earning big fees.

After Reeves had finished speaking, the judge droned on, instructing the jury. Olivia tuned him out, her thoughts returning to Sissy and Dr. Bella. She was optimistic that Reeves could be some help to Sissy and the Bella family in keeping the matter quiet.

The judge had departed. The bailiff ordered everyone to rise. Olivia stood up, eager now to make her presence known to Reeves. The jury filed out to go and begin their deliberation. On his feet beside his client, Reeves turned to face the tiered seating gallery, but his gaze didn't reach her.

A small group of people were in the first row behind the mahogany railing. His attention was on them. They made their way down onto the floor of the courtroom and clustered around May Pickens, obviously friends or family there to support her.

Reeves was still facing in her direction. Olivia took a step down the aisle, holding out her hand. He raised his head and saw her.

"Olivia." He spoke her name in surprise, his expression puzzled and concerned. While he was collecting his briefcase, he said a few quick words to his client and then made his way quickly up into the gallery. "Why are you here?" he asked when he was several steps away. "Has something happened?"

Olivia felt foolish at having to explain why she'd taken off from work and rushed downtown to the courthouse. She waited until he had reached her to answer. "Something upsetting has come up. I had lunch with Sissy today. Her father is being sued for malpractice and..." Her voice stuck in her throat. It wasn't necessary to go on. Reeves looked sick with guilty understanding. "Please, tell me that what I'm thinking is wrong," she whispered. "You aren't the attorney, are you?"

He cursed helplessly under his breath. "I was going to tell you everything about the Bella lawsuit tonight."

She shook her head slowly, gazing at him, the pain in her chest making tears come to her eyes. "The woman who called your condo that Sunday was the wife of Dr. Bella's patient." The same Sunday they'd made love for the first time. "Now I understand why you ran to pick up the phone."

Reeves clasped her shoulder. "Let's go somewhere less public and talk."

Olivia pushed his hand away. "Please don't touch me."

He let his hand drop. The defeated motion made something break inside her. "Where is your conscience, Reeves? How could you be so double-faced? Allowing me to believe that I could trust you when all the time you were secretly handling a lawsuit against my friend's father! That's despicable! I'll never forgive you!"

His broad shoulders sagged at her words. The lack of any defense only deepened her despair.

"My conscience was my downfall, Olivia. Please, you have to hear my side of it."

"There's nothing to hear. No other side to see," she said dully. "The whole time I was learning to trust you, you weren't being open and honest with me. You let me fall in love with a figment of my imagination."

Her words hurt him. It took him a second to reply. "I hated not being open and aboveboard about the Bella case, but I just didn't dare. I was afraid of losing you. I knew that you would react just the way you are reacting. Tonight I was going to tell you everything, including the fact that I can't in conscience refer my client to another attorney, as I was intending to do."

"Your sister will be proud of you anyway," Olivia said bitterly. "Maybe she can do a news report to finish up the job on Dr. Bella's reputation."

"If you knew the circumstances, Olivia, maybe you could understand my sense of obligation to my client."

"It's not your duty as an attorney that's in question here, Reeves. You betrayed my trust, proved once again how undependable my instincts about men are."

"Truly I'm sorry," he said bleakly. "My only excuse is that I fell in love with you and was afraid of losing you. You affected me the way a magnet affects a compass, throwing off my sense of direction, my judgement. I wanted to be the man you wanted me to be, but it wouldn't have worked for either of us in the long run." His tone was full of regret and futility, and he was using past tense.

"I only wanted you to be the man I thought you were, the man you've turned out not to be."

"Will you see me tonight? Let me explain the whole sequence?"

"No, I won't see you tonight or any other night or ever again. And please don't call me, because I don't want to talk to you. What can you say to change anything?" He wasn't even fighting for their relationship. He'd obviously conceded that it was over.

"You can't just say goodbye and walk away, Olivia," he protested.

"It's over between us, Reeves. Let's just part with some dignity."

He stared at her, as though searching for some weakening. Then he stood taller, squaring his slumped shoulders, some inner resolution reflected in his posture.

"First I'm taking you somewhere. There are some people I want you to meet."

"I'm not going anywhere with you or meeting any people."

"Yes, you are. Come on."

He took her arm in a firm grip. When Olivia pushed at his hand, he tightened his fingers into a vise. This was a Reeves reminiscent of the boy and the young man, hard and determined and impervious to her will.

After a brief struggle with herself, Olivia accompanied him without any further objection. In the outside corridor and riding down in the elevator, he encountered acquaintances and briefly acknowledged greetings, not introducing her.

They didn't speak to each other again until they were in his car. Olivia broke the strained silence. "Where are you taking me?"

"To Baptist Hospital," he answered tersely.

The leather of the seat in his Porsche felt cold. The leather scent mingling with the scent of his after-shave was unendurably familiar.

This was her last ride in his car with him.

"Who is it that you want me to meet at Baptist Hospital?"

"Rachel Wade and her son and daughter. Dr. Bella's patient that he butchered, Bill Wade, is in intensive care there."

"You mean the operation left him in critical condition?" she asked, horrified.

"The operation left him an invalid. The gun he put to his head this weekend almost finished up the butchering job Dr. Bella did on him."

"Oh, God, *no,*" Olivia murmured in dismay. "Poor man. Poor Sissy. She's going to feel so *awful,* knowing her father is responsible...."

Reeves's glance was hard and unsympathetic. "How bad Sissy feels is nothing compared to what Bill Wade's wife is going through. What his children are going through. And there's no happy ending to the story, whether he lives or dies. Either way, Rachel has lost a husband, and her kids have lost a father."

"It's tragic for everyone concerned, including Dr. Bella. Imagine the guilt of having accidentally ruined another human being's life. What a terrible thing for Dr. Bella and his wife and family, too." Couldn't he see that side of the tragedy?

"Bella's life won't be shortened unless he drinks himself into the grave faster," Reeves replied, unmoved. "His life-style won't be noticeably affected even if this lawsuit accomplishes what it should accomplish and forces him into retirement. He'll live just as well."

"That doesn't mean he'll sleep well or be at peace with himself. Would your sense of justice be better served if Dr. Bella were reduced to being a pauper?"

When he didn't answer, Olivia turned her head and gazed dully out the window.

"I won't be joining Duplantis & Duplantis," he said. "I meant to tell you that tonight, too."

"You've had a change of heart about a lot of things, it seems." Her remark was quietly bitter.

"I would be a rich man's attorney, and that's not the right kind of law practice for me."

"Then you should continue your present law practice. You'll be burning your bridges with Duplantis & Duplantis anyway with this lawsuit, I should think.

William's father and Dr. Bella are longtime friends. You'll be closing a lot of doors, Reeves. The Bellas have many friends."

"I realize that I won't be receiving any more invitations to the Hymers' summer home in Pass Christian," he replied, deep regret in his voice. "And membership in New Orleans Country Club is out the window. But those are things I can live without. It's giving up my fantasy about a life with you that's really hard, Olivia."

"No harder than it is for me to give up my fantasy about living happily ever after with you, Reeves. I had us moved into a house in the Garden District and was picking out names for our children."

"I wish like hell that I could have been the right man for you."

"So do I."

They rode in silence, carrying out his mission that wouldn't heal their destroyed relationship.

"You didn't forget to call last night," she stated.

He sighed. "No, I didn't forget."

At the hospital he parked and reached to turn off the engine. Olivia touched his hand to stop him, making the briefest possible contact.

"What's the point, Reeves? Your client's wife has my complete sympathy. In light of what she is going through, it's hardly considerate to drag in a total stranger."

He shifted the car into gear and backed out.

Olivia's emotions suddenly got the best of her, tears welling up and spilling down her cheeks, she turned her head away from him while she felt in her purse for a tissue.

He cursed under his breath.

"I'm sorry." She gulped. She blew her nose, using the tissue, and cleared her throat. "I know how you men hate weepy women. I'm dreading telling Sissy that you're the attorney representing her father's patient. Of all the ironies, she asked me to ask you for your help in resolving the whole tragic mess without any scandal."

"I'll call Sissy and tell her myself. I'll make it clear that you had no knowledge until this afternoon."

"No, she's my friend. I'll break the news. It's bad news aside from personal reasons. I doubt Dr. Bella can hire an attorney as good as you are."

"He'll have several attorneys as good as I am. But thanks for the compliment," he added uncertainly.

"You're welcome."

The conversation lapsed again.

They were several minutes away from the courthouse when he said earnestly, "There's no intent on my part to hurt Sissy or Mrs. Bella or even punish Dr. Bella, for that matter. My purpose is to ensure that Bill Wade's family is provided for financially and, if possible, to bar Bella from the operating room. I can't accomplish the latter goal without public knowledge of his incompetence."

"Maybe you can, if you really looked for a way. Maybe it isn't necessary to expose Sissy and her mother to public humiliation. Your problem, Reeves, is that you've reserved your compassion for the less fortunate innocent people involved."

"If I were to find a way—and I'm doubtful I could— it still wouldn't make any difference with us, would it?"

"I'd be grateful, but that's all."

He nodded, his expression deeply disheartened.

At the entrance to the parking lot where she'd left her car, Olivia unbuckled her seat belt and looked at him, tears of anguish threatening. "Goodbye," she said thickly, and got out. If he spoke any word of parting before she slammed the door, she didn't hear him.

Chapter Thirteen

"Here's your picture in the society pages. Standing next to you is Dr. Ned Barton." Judy was reading the caption. "Is he married? If he is, he's in trouble with his wife. The camera caught him looking at you like he could eat you with a spoon." She tossed the section of newspaper over to Olivia, who glanced at the picture with little interest.

The same lack of interest was in her voice as she replied, "He isn't married. He's one of George DeMarco's medical partners."

"In the picture he looks attractive."

"He is an attractive man and quite personable." Olivia was looking at the other pictures of guests at the big retirement party for Dr. Bella that she'd attended the previous evening. "This is a nice picture of Dr. and Mrs. Bella and Sissy and George."

"Did Dr. Bella manage to stay on the wagon?"

"He held a glass of club soda all night. His hand was so shaky that the ice cubes rattled."

"And you couldn't help thinking that he'd held a scalpel."

Olivia nodded. She also hadn't been able to keep from thinking about Reeves all night. Three months had gone by since she'd last seen him and said goodbye to him.

He *had* found a way to spare the Bella family public exposure. Through Sissy, Olivia knew that he'd negotiated a huge settlement with Dr. Bella's insurance company. A condition of the settlement, fully supported by wife and daughter, had been that Dr. Bella retire from medicine. There hadn't been a breath of scandal.

Olivia wanted to thank Reeves.

"Was the party any fun?" Judy asked with a determined cheerfulness.

"It was good to see Marcia and Clinton and some of my other old friends, but no, the party *wasn't* fun. I felt sad that Dr. Bella's medical career had had to end like that, on a note of tragedy." Bill Wade, Dr. Bella's patient, had died in the hospital, following his suicide attempt. "There was very little real cause for celebration. But at least the whole world doesn't know it. Sissy and her mother can suffer their disillusionment in private."

"Like you were unable to do because of Doreen."

"Like I was unable to do."

"This whole business with Dr. Bella brought it all back, didn't it?"

"Yes. It brought back the anger and the sense of betrayal. But last night I realized that a lot of my anger was really regret. Seeing how supportive Sissy and Mrs. Bella are, it came home to me that I wished I could have been there somehow for my grandfather in his blackest hour and prevented his suicide."

Judy sighed, obviously depressed by the conversation. "Is there any bright side? Any possible happy ending to your story, Olivia?"

Olivia's smile was wan. "Only one, and it's not very probable."

"Why don't you see Reeves and talk to him? Maybe he's as miserable as you are."

"Last night I came so close to trying to call him," Olivia confessed. "But I knew that I'd just get his answering machine. He wouldn't have been home on a Saturday night. By now I'm sure he's dating someone else."

"He might not be. You're not dating anyone. You haven't been on a single date in three months. Did this Dr. Ned Barton ask you out?"

"He asked if I would go out with him."

"And?" Judy gestured, pulling out an answer.

"I wasn't encouraging," Olivia admitted.

"Is it pride keeping you from trying to make up with Reeves?"

"No, it's lack of confidence. He gave up so easily, Judy. He didn't make any effort to salvage our relationship. That tells me that he really didn't love me. I was just a brief infatuation for him. My main attraction was a superficial glamour."

"It surprises me that he wasn't more persistent," Judy conceded. "Reeves strikes me as a more determined type."

"He has tremendous drive and determination." Olivia's sigh was despondent. "Look how he wouldn't take no for an answer when he was first trying to date me."

"I've seen the man look at you. He worshiped you. There has to be some other explanation for the way he let you break off with him."

"What other explanation can there be?" Beneath her skepticism, Olivia was pathetically eager, wanting to grasp at straws.

"Maybe he was never really convinced that your love for him was the kind that lasts through thick and thin. Maybe his whole problem is lack of confidence."

"He's the most confident man I've ever known."

"You told him that you never wanted to see him again. He might have believed you." Judy pointed to the society section of the newspaper. "You hide a lot beneath that polished exterior, Olivia. If Reeves sees that picture of you and the nice-looking doctor, he won't detect any evidence of a broken heart."

"I want to see him, but I'm a coward." With those words, Olivia stood up, letting the pages of newspaper slide to the carpet.

"Are you going to call him now?" Judy inquired worriedly as Olivia headed for the stairs.

"No, I'm going to go to his condo and talk to him in person."

She had to know the worst and get on with life.

Olivia no longer had a key to Reeves's condo. She'd returned it and the key to the building by insured mail without a note. Sending off the package, she was denied access once again to her old home.

After parking her car at the Prescott mansion, she got out, unnerved by the necessity for buzzing Reeves's condo and announcing her presence outside. As if on cue, another car drove in with a man behind the wheel. She glanced at it, thinking that if the driver were an occupant, she might wait and enter with him.

He obviously was an occupant. Using a remote device, he opened one of the garage doors and parked his car inside. *He'd opened Reeves's garage.* Olivia had just registered that puzzling fact when she recognized Alan Cramer as the man emerging, dressed in tennis clothes and carrying a tennis bag with racket handles protruding. Apparently he'd played an early-morning match because his shirt was damp with perspiration and a soiled towel trailed from the bag.

Was he house-sitting? She prepared herself for the disappointing discovery that Reeves was out of town on a trip.

"Olivia. Well, hello there." Alan greeted her with mild surprise. Driving in, he would have had a chance to spot her.

"Hi, Alan. How are you?"

"I'm just fine." He had reached her car. "How are you?" Polite curiosity was written on his face.

"I'm fine, too. I came to see Reeves."

His eyebrows shot up, and he looked totally befuddled for a second or two. "You do know that Reeves has moved?"

"Moved?" she repeated foolishly.

"He sold his condo to me."

"I didn't know. We haven't been in touch."

"Reeves mentioned that you'd broken off with him. Could I offer you some coffee?" Alan asked hospitably.

"Thank you, no." Olivia was having trouble taking in the news that Reeves had sold his condo and was living somewhere else. "Can you tell me his new address?"

"Sure. It's only five minutes from here. He stayed in the uptown area." He told her the street name and number.

"That must not be a condo in that neighborhood."

"No, it isn't. He bought an old-fashioned duplex this time. Stucco exterior with a tile roof. He lives upstairs and rents the downstairs to tenants. Real nice place but totally different. Big, high-ceilinged rooms."

"I may go by there and see if he's home," she said uncertainly, giving Alan a chance to dissuade her. He would probably know if Reeves was involved with another woman, who might be spending the weekend.

"By all means, do go by," he replied. "If you don't find him there, he's probably at his office. You know the address, on Gravier Street?"

"Yes, I know it. Thanks, Alan."

He smiled his wry, attractive smile. His blue eyes glinted with a kindly light as well as keen intelligence. "Sure thing."

"How's Kay?" she asked out of politeness.

"She was doing great the last time I ran into her. That was about a month ago," he added with a sigh.

"I'm sorry."

"No need to be sorry. It was a congenial parting of the ways. But if you had a sister, I would definitely be interested."

"Especially if she was a blonde?"

He grinned.

"I have a blond apartment mate who's almost like a sister."

"Then patch things up with Talbot, and the four of us will go out together real soon."

"That would be fun," Olivia said with as much despair as wistfulness. The date wasn't at all likely to ever materialize.

Reeves's move to another location in the same general vicinity was easy to interpret. He'd wanted a new place to live, free of any associations with her, distant or recent.

Olivia easily found his house in a quiet, dignified neighborhood with handsome, well-maintained two-story homes built in a more gracious era. A few had been originally designed to be duplexes, like his. Others perhaps had been modified on the interior to form two or even three spacious apartments, but the majority were large single-family dwellings occupied by professionals and others in high-earning occupations.

Most of the exteriors were white with sober contrasting trim. His house was painted a cream color. Its terra-cotta tiled roof, the genuine dated article, lent the building a Mediterranean air. One entrance had a small elegant portico while the other was tucked away and less noticeable. To the casual eye, the house wouldn't be identifiable as a duplex, which had been the architect's intention.

She instinctively approved his choice, knew without even viewing his upstairs apartment that she would like it much better than his condo, which, in truth, she wouldn't have liked even in another condo building. It had been too sleek, too trendy for her taste.

I hope a previous owner hasn't overmodernized the interior, she reflected and then was struck by despondence. She might never see the interior. If Reeves were home, he might not invite her inside.

A paved driveway led to a double garage at the rear of the house. The door was closed, making it impossible to tell whether his Porsche was parked safely out of sight. That is, if he still owned the Porsche. Maybe he'd gotten a different car, too, one she'd never ridden in.

With little more to sustain her than a kind of dogged courage, Olivia pulled into the driveway. Getting out, she slammed her car door briskly and walked on shaky legs along a sidewalk to the steps leading up to the porticoed entrance. The sound of her footsteps seemed to make dents in the pervasive quietness.

Standing on the sheltered stoop, she peered through the glass panes of the door into a foyer that was also a stairwell. This was Reeves's entrance since he lived upstairs.

The foyer floor was varnished wood, waxed but bare of a rug. The staircase had a graceful banister and carved spindles, both a darker wood than the floor, probably mahogany. Not a single picture was in evidence. Not a stick of furniture. Somehow the stark bareness was reassuring. At least there wasn't a woman's touch.

Olivia pressed the doorbell. While she waited nervously, she tapped the toe of a lilac sandal that matched her lilac sundress.

No footsteps were audible. All was quiet. Pressing the button again, she put her ear close to the door and heard a faint chiming sound. The doorbell worked.

Reeves must not be home.

Now what should she do?

Overwhelmed by disappointment, she suddenly couldn't deal with deciding her next move. Her whole plan to visit him unannounced seemed terribly ill conceived.

Descending several steps, she sat down dejectedly on the concrete coping, painted the same cream color as the house. A plaintive meow drew her attention. Glancing in the direction of the sound, she saw a huge marmalade cat was ambling lazily across the lawn from next door, coming to visit her.

"Hello there," Olivia greeted the cat in a disheartened tone. "Are you the welcoming committee?"

Her answer was another meow. Moving at its own stately pace, the cat reached the steps and mounted them to perch daintily near her feet. Olivia bent over and crooned to the feline as she stroked its long silky fur.

After two or three minutes of evident enjoyment of the petting, the cat yawned, stretched and ambled back to its own yard. A bemused smile on her lips, Olivia watched the languid departure.

Not having glimpsed another human being, she didn't feel conspicuous, sitting on Reeves's doorstep. But that changed instantly as she turned her head and saw him approaching on foot.

He'd obviously been out jogging and was returning, wearing jogging shorts and a sweat-stained cropped T-shirt that molded his broad shoulders and muscular chest, leaving a band of taut stomach bare. He'd spotted her first. With a sinking heart, Olivia noted the absence of any welcome on his face.

What was she doing here? his expression seemed to ask.

"Hello, Reeves." She greeted him, summoning her poise.

"Hello, Olivia."

He strode along the sidewalk toward the steps.

"I was trying to decide whether to persevere in my attempt to track you down," she explained.

"Here I am," he said. For a second, Olivia thought that he intended to stand at the foot of the steps and let her say her piece, but then he sat down on the coping across from her.

His physical nearness made a powerful impact on her senses. He was so vital, so masculine. Olivia gazed at him hungrily while he stripped off the red bandanna, which he wore for a headband, and wiped his face and neck of perspiration. The urge to touch him was so strong that she clenched her hands around her small purse.

"I admire your fortitude, jogging in this humidity," she ventured as he crumpled the bandanna into a tight ball and held it in one big hand.

He shrugged aside the remark, inspecting her from head to toe. "I don't have to ask how you're doing," he said. "I can see for myself."

"I don't know what you see," she replied, "but I haven't exactly had the best summer of my life."

"It doesn't show. You're looking as beautiful as ever." Judging from his tone and expression, he took no pleasure in her appearance anymore.

"Last night was Dr. Bella's retirement party. I attended it—"

"I read this morning's paper," he interrupted tersely. "I saw the pictures."

"I wanted to tell you how grateful I am over the way you handled the malpractice lawsuit."

He rubbed the back of his neck with the balled-up bandanna. The motion was impatient. "No thanks are necessary. The way I handled the lawsuit was best for all concerned, including my client. His family wasn't put through the ordeal of a trial."

"Well, I'd like to say thank you anyway." Even though he hadn't acted out of any consideration for her, a fact he wanted to impress upon her.

Olivia's pride told her that she should collect her shredded dignity and go, but instead she kept her seat. "I went to your condo on St. Charles," she said. "I had no inkling that you'd moved. Alan drove up, looking very surprised to see me. He gave me your new address.

It's a very handsome house, by the way. And the neighborhood is nice."

"The house is a duplex," he volunteered.

"Alan told me that it was."

"I live upstairs."

Olivia nodded. The sound of his voice was such music to her ears, even with his brusque, unfriendly note.

"The rooms are large," he said. "My furniture gets lost. It's totally inappropriate, of course, the wrong style. I plan to replace it all, as soon as I can get around to it."

With new furniture that she wouldn't see or enjoy with him. A huge lump formed in her throat at the thought. Not trusting her voice, she nodded again, trying to smile.

"I'll probably hire a decorator," he stated.

A more likely scenario was that he would end up getting free decorating help from a woman who would live in the house with him.

Misery welled up inside Olivia, bringing the sudden threat of tears. Reeves didn't look or sound happy, but neither was he interested in reconciling with her. That was clearly obvious. What he wanted was for her to leave.

"Well, I'd better go," she said, making a show of consulting her watch as though she had an appointment.

"No, don't let me keep you," he answered curtly. "You'll be late for your lunch date."

They both stood up. Olivia started to correct his error, but a glaze of tears were burning her eyes. If she stayed any longer, she would break down and sob her heart out right in front of him.

"Goodbye," she said thickly, negotiating the remaining steps down to the sidewalk. Hot tears were pouring down her cheeks as she headed for her car, a blurry object in his driveway.

How she would manage to see well enough to drive was questionable, but somehow Olivia would get several blocks away, out of sight. Her immediate goal was simply to reach the car, the most direct route being a shortcut across the lawn. As soon as she had veered off the sidewalk, Olivia realized that she'd made a mistake. The tiny heels of her sandals dug into the thick green turf, making haste difficult.

All she needed was to go sprawling and make a total spectacle of herself. The panicky thought had no more than flashed through her mind when her right foot, bearing her weight, twisted. Fighting for balance, she flailed her arms and cried out helplessly. Losing the battle with gravity, she fell backward, landing hard in a sitting position and jarring the breath from her lungs.

"Olivia!" Reeves was there immediately, kneeling beside her on the grass. "Are you hurt?"

She buried her face in her hands and sobbed a denial. "No, I'm not hurt."

"Are you sure?"

"Please. Just go inside and give me some privacy," she begged.

"Let me help you to your car." His hands were gentle and strong on her shoulders.

"No, I'll just sit here a moment. I don't need any help."

He sighed heavily. "Please don't cry like that," he implored gruffly.

"I'm *sor*-ry," she apologized, sobbing harder. "I shouldn't have come."

"If you sit there too long, you'll get a grass stain on your pretty dress." His hands came down to clasp her waist. "Come on. Help me get you on your feet."

"Ruining my dress is the least of my worries." She wiped her face with her hands, making an effort to compose herself.

"You do have a date, don't you?" he asked.

"No, I don't have a date."

"What about the doctor you were with at the Bella retirement party?"

"I wasn't with him. He was just there."

"You aren't dating him?"

Olivia sniffled. The interrogation was drying up her tears. "I went to the party by myself. I'm not dating anyone."

Reeves rocked back on his heels, taking his hands away from her waist.

"The way he was looking at you in that damned picture—I thought..."

"You thought wrong. I haven't gone out on any dates since we broke up." She gathered her nerve. "Have you?"

"No."

Olivia curled sideways, sitting more gracefully and facing him. He sat back on the grass, too, looking sober and guarded, but much more approachable than he had earlier.

"I didn't come just to thank you on Sissy's behalf," she confessed. "I wanted to see you."

"It was a shock finding you here," he replied. "Earlier I had opened up the newspaper and seen the picture of you with another guy. It was like a fist in my gut."

"I've never felt any more unwelcome than when I saw your expression today."

His shrug was both defense and apology. "You were dressed so pretty, sitting there on my doorstep. My first thought was that you probably had a brunch date with him and had stopped by on your way to meet him."

"I wore this dress to visit you."

"You were smiling to yourself about something."

"Your neighbor's cat had come over to pay a call and cheered me up a little. It threw me for a loop to learn from Alan that you'd up and sold your condo."

"I'd approached him about selling it to him even before everything went to hell between us."

"You had?"

"I didn't mention it because you'd reacted so negatively to my getting another place. I wanted us to live together somewhere else. The fresh-start theory. My plan was for you to have some input in picking out the new place, but things didn't work out that way."

"I like the one you picked out yourself."

"You haven't seen the inside yet."

"Could I see it?"

He got to his feet and reached down his hand. Olivia took it and he helped her up.

"Just don't expect too much," he warned.

"I'm sure I'll like it." She winced as she took a step, still holding his hand.

"You did hurt your ankle," he said, his arm immediately going around her. "Put your arm around my waist and let me support your weight."

"It's not my ankle. It's my hip joints," she corrected him. Nevertheless she followed his instructions, taking both pleasure and comfort in her dependency.

His actions said he still cared for her.

Chapter Fourteen

"Do you have hardwood floors upstairs, too?" she asked as they entered the foyer. The air-conditioned coolness felt wonderful.

"Except for the two bathrooms. The kitchen even has a wooden floor," Reeves replied, closing and locking the door. Side by side they started up the stairs, taking them slowly, his arm around her and her arm around him. "Without carpeting, the place echoes like a gymnasium. I walk around in my socks out of consideration for my downstairs tenant."

"You'll need some large area rugs."

"I was thinking that Oriental rugs might look nice." He glanced at her for her reaction.

"You can't go wrong with Oriental rugs. You can decorate a room around a gorgeous Persian or Chinese rug."

"Pick it out first and go from there? It's the sequence of selecting everything that goes into a room that's mind-boggling," he confessed.

"I would be glad to go browsing with you in furniture stores. I don't think you'd be happy hiring a decorator. You want your home to make a statement about *your* taste and personality, not some other person's. It should suit your life-style."

He didn't respond. Olivia felt rebuffed not to be taken up on her offer to give him free decorating advice.

"Of course, that's my opinion," she said. "You may feel different."

"No, I agree with you in principle. A home should suit those who live in it." He added, "The word *abode,* more than *home,* fits the places where I've lived since I moved out on my own."

"I suppose that's true of the average young, single person. Single man, especially."

They had reached a long landing at the top of the stairs, directly over the foyer. Natural light from two tall windows made it a delightful space. Olivia could visualize a narrow rug on the floor. Mentally she placed a graceful wrought-iron bench, a ficus tree in a porcelain planter, some original watercolors on the walls.

"Very nice," she said.

Reeves shot her a dubious glance. "The living room," he announced unnecessarily, ushering her through the open doorway at the end. He steered her over to his black leather sofa set along the inside wall. "Why don't you make yourself comfortable while I take a shower and change. I won't be long."

Olivia gazed after him wistfully. Her status seemed purely and simply guest in his house.

Instead of sitting on the sofa, she stood where he'd left her and surveyed the room, admiring it's potential for elegance. It was beautifully proportioned, spacious and high-ceilinged, with more of those graceful tall windows along the two outside walls. An ornate brass-and-crystal light fixture hung from the center of a lovely plaster medallion.

An archway afforded a glimpse into the adjoining room. Giving in to her curiosity, Olivia decided to take a tour on her own. Probably Reeves wouldn't object. Walking from room to room, she grew more and more enthusiastic about the house's charm. Between the dining room and the kitchen was a butler's pantry with storage cabinets. The kitchen was modern and well equipped, but not space-age.

Venturing farther, she glanced into two unfurnished bedrooms and a bathroom. To her delight, the latter still had the original white marble mosaic tile. The white fixtures were undoubtedly the original ones, too. Instead of a vanity, there was a porcelain pedestal sink with brass taps. The capacious claw-footed tub had been adapted to double as a shower. No shower curtain had been hung yet, nor were any towels in sight. The bathroom was clean and empty, like most of the rooms.

Heading back down the hallway, Olivia could see the open door to Reeves's bedroom. Through the door she glimpsed his bed. Dared she be so bold as to enter instead of returning to the living room?

The woman in her said *yes*.

In the doorway she gazed at his familiar furnishings, noting that the bed had been made up, but hastily. The comforter hung slightly askew. It was an endearing and encouraging thought that he might have paused to tidy up his bedroom before taking his shower. On impulse she went over and did a neater job. Straightening from fluffing his pillow, she realized that he was watching her, standing in the door of an adjoining bathroom wearing only a towel.

"I hope you don't mind," she said, flustered and embarrassed. "I took myself on a tour of your house, and it ended here in your bedroom."

"What's the verdict?" he asked.

"The verdict?" His choice of words made her smile. "You make it sound as though I'm a one-woman jury."

"You are, for all practical purposes."

She sat down on the side of his bed, feeling more confident by the moment. Finding her in his bedroom wasn't objectionable for him.

"At this moment I'd rather be a woman judge," she said. "Then I would move this process along. No wonder trials take so long. You lawyers are a slow, cautious lot."

"What exactly is it that you'd like to speed up?"

"Making up with you."

She patted the bed next to her. He came over and sat beside her, the bed sinking beneath his weight.

"Kiss me. *Please,*" she requested.

His response wasn't reluctant, nor was it tentative. He lifted his hand and framed her cheek, his touch tender, reverent, *loving*. Gripped by poignant emotion, Olivia gazed into his eyes as he brought his mouth to hers.

They kissed lingeringly, the contact answering a thousand complex questions and bringing sublime reassurance. Her arms crept up around his neck.

"I missed you so much," she whispered, when they pulled apart to gaze into each other's eyes again.

"I missed you," he said, his voice low and fervent. He touched her hair, her face with his fingertips as though assuring himself that she was really there and not a mirage.

"Can we start over, Reeves? And this time not have any secrets?"

"There's nothing in the world I want more than having a life with you, Olivia."

He kissed her again tenderly.

"How soon?" she asked when they drew apart.

"How soon?" he repeated, uncertain of her meaning.

"How soon can we begin having a life together? We've lost three whole months, being apart."

"As far as I'm concerned, you could move in with me immediately. But I realize that you'll want to wait until the place is furnished better and decorated."

"You realize wrong." Olivia stroked his cheek. "I would move in with you if you were renting a studio apartment with a Hide-A-Bed to sleep in. My motivation is *not* to live in greater luxury, but to live with the man I love...*you.*"

His arms came around her, and he hugged her so tightly that the air was squeezed from her lungs. "I love you," he said. "And I just knew I'd lost you. In my heart I never believed that you could be mine." His embrace eased enough so that she could breathe. "Do you really like the house? Tell me honestly."

"I really *really* like it."

"You can have a free hand. Fix it up to suit you."

"To suit *us,* you and me. I want it to be a place where we can invite close friends like Alan and Judy. Those two will probably be our first dinner guests. Maybe by Christmas we'll have things in good enough shape to throw a party and send out invitations to everybody we know, including Doreen. Whether she comes or not is up to her." A small reflex of surprise ran through his body. Before he could say anything, she went on.

"If your parents haven't visited us before then, they might want to make a trip to New Orleans for the holidays. We'll certainly have plenty of room with two extra bedrooms and a second bathroom. Am I going too fast for you?"

He had pulled back to search her face questioningly as though unsure of what he was hearing.

"No, I'm keeping pace. Just barely. Go on."

Olivia took in a deep breath. "Maybe at this party, where our friends and acquaintances are gathered, we might announce the news that we're planning to get married. Of course, that might be rushing matters for you."

"It wouldn't be rushing matters for me if we put an announcement in the newspaper tomorrow. Surely you know that."

"How could I know that? You haven't mentioned a word about marriage, only about living together."

"You want to get married?"

"My biggest ambition is becoming Mrs. Reeves Talbot. Please get around to proposing soon."

He was taking in the import of her softly spoken confession. Olivia could read in his expression that gladness was spreading through him and turning to jubilation. His hands caressed her back, and he glanced downward at himself, as though suddenly conscious of his state of undress.

"Somehow in my wildest imaginings, I never thought that I would propose marriage to the woman I love when I was wearing nothing but a towel," he said with husky amusement. Any hint of uncertainty had turned to possessiveness.

"You could always take the towel off," Olivia suggested with a seductive smile. "Or I could take it off for you since you're busy."

He was unzipping her sundress. She attended to unwrapping the towel and came into intimate contact with his aroused, tumescent body, the body of her future husband.

That thrilling knowledge made fondling him more than physical pleasure. It gave passion a whole deeper meaning.

Even taking precautions later in the stage of their lovemaking when they were both wild with desire had a new wonderful significance because of that time in the future when they would dispense with birth control.

Helping him with the condom, Olivia said, "I want to have children."

"So do I," he assured her.

When he entered her, he wasn't just the man she loved, the man she would wed, but also the man who would father their children. She had a special awareness of his virility, a special joy in her own womanhood.

Satisfaction was deep and complete.

Lying in Reeves's arms, Olivia was filled with anticipation for their life together.

"I'm going to love living here in this house, in this neighborhood," she mused happily. "I won't mind commuting to Metairie until I find another job downtown."

"If you want to keep on working, that's fine with me, but we won't need your salary," Reeves said. "I earn a large enough income to support the two of us. Then you could reschedule the bridge party for your elderly ladies to a weekday instead of Saturday. I assume that you won't be discontinuing that obligation."

"Oh, no. I wouldn't have the heart. And I've gotten involved in a couple of other volunteer projects during the last three months. I was so miserable and needed to do worthwhile activities to get my mind off myself. Now I can't just drop them because there are those who are depending on me."

"I can understand that. What are the projects?"

She explained that one was a fashion show fund-raiser for a Metairie school. The models would be high school students enrolled in the school.

"It's turned into more than I bargained for," Olivia admitted. "I agreed to be modeling coach and am ending up conducting a charm school. But the teenagers are fun and they will benefit if I can teach them some poise and pride in their appearance. No matter what anyone says to the contrary, developing good posture, wearing clothes well and generally appearing confident *are* important because how the world reacts to us affects our performance."

"I couldn't agree more."

"You should agree. You're a prime example. In fact, I may just bribe you into a guest appearance to inspire my boys."

"The only bribe I need is taking the fashion coach home with me afterward," he said, gathering her a little closer to him. Then he added earnestly, "Actually I'm flattered as hell."

"Be serious!" she chided. "You're a walking advertisement of the well-groomed, well-dressed male. You carry yourself like the natural athlete you are. You're courteous with men. Around women you have a touch of courtliness that we just eat up. You can handle yourself in any social situation." Once she'd gotten started, Olivia had warmed to her subject.

"In other words you can take me anywhere and not worry about my embarrassing you."

Wriggling into a more upright position that allowed her to gaze into his face, she verified that he *hadn't* spoken entirely tongue-in-cheek.

"No, that's not stating it right. You can take *me* anywhere and I'm proud to be with you. *We* can go anywhere together."

"Anywhere we're invited. Marrying me and being my wife can never bring you the perks that you would have enjoyed if you'd married William Duplantis."

"Reeves, don't you realize how proud I'll be of you? You're bright and successful. That day I watched you in court, I couldn't have been more impressed. You're a man I can admire and have faith in. Years ago I could have married back into New Orleans society if that had been important to me, but it isn't."

"Fortunately for me," he said huskily. "Will you marry me, Olivia? If you will, I'll try never to let you down."

She smiled through a haze of happy tears. "Yes, I'll marry you, Reeves."

They shared a long vulnerable moment and then kissed, sealing their contract for a life together.

Olivia lay in his close embrace again. "Remember, no secrets," she said. "We'll air our insecurities from now on and eliminate emotional guesswork."

"We'll communicate," he agreed. "I'll start by telling you that I have reservations about your continuing to work after we're married. It would suit me much better if you quit your job and devoted your time to homemaking and your volunteer work and to me. We'll be wanting to start a family in a year or two so it would only be a matter of time anyway before you gave up working. Why stretch yourself thin in the meanwhile?'' He paused hesitantly, giving her a chance to react.

''If I seemed quiet,'' Olivia said, a smile in her voice, ''I was imagining cleaning out my desk and rehearsing a speech for the party my co-workers will give me on my last day at work. I've never pretended to be a career woman. Please go on.''

And he did.

*   *   *   *   *

Silhouette SPECIAL EDITION

It takes a very special man to win

That SPECIAL Woman!

She's friend, wife, mother—she's you! And beside each Special Woman stands a wonderfully *special* man. It's a celebration of our heroines—and the men who become part of their lives.

Look for these exciting titles from Silhouette Special Edition:

January   BUILDING DREAMS by Ginna Gray

February   HASTY WEDDING by Debbie Macomber

March   THE AWAKENING by Patricia Coughlin

April   FALLING FOR RACHEL by Nora Roberts

Don't miss THAT SPECIAL WOMAN! each month—from some of your special authors! Only from Silhouette Special Edition! And for the most special woman of all—you, our loyal reader— we have a wonderful gift: a beautiful journal to record all of your special moments. Look for details in this month's THAT SPECIAL WOMAN! title, available at your favorite retail outlet.

TSW1R

Take 4 bestselling love stories FREE
Plus get a FREE surprise gift!

Silhouette®
SPECIAL EDITION®

COMING NEXT MONTH

#805 TRUE BLUE HEARTS—Curtiss Ann Matlock
Rough-and-tumble cowboy Rory Breen and mother of two
Zoe Yarberry knew that getting together was unwise. But
though their heads were telling them no, their hearts...

#806 HARDWORKING MAN—Gina Ferris
Family Found
The first time private investigator Cassie Browning met
Jared Walker, he was in jail. Cassie soon discovered that
clearing Jared's name and reuniting him with his family
were easier tasks than fighting her feelings for him!

#807 YOUR CHILD, MY CHILD—Jennifer Mikels
When confirmed bachelor Pete Hogan opened his door to
Anne LeClare and her child, he thought he was saving them
from a snowstorm. But the forecast quickly changed to sunny
skies when they offered him the chance for love.

#808 LIVE, LAUGH, LOVE—Ada Steward
Jesse Carder had traveled far to rekindle the flames of an old
love—until she met sexy Dillon Ruiz. Dillon brought Jesse's
thoughts back to the present, but was their future possible?

#809 MAN OF THE FAMILY—Andrea Edwards
Tough cop Mike Minelli had seen Angie Hartman on the screen as
a former horror movie queen! Now he sensed vulnerable Angie
was hiding more than bad acting in her past!

#810 FALLING FOR RACHEL—Nora Roberts
That Special Woman!
Career-minded Rachel Stanislaski had little time for matters of the
heart. But when handsome Zackary Muldoon entered her life,
Rachel's pulse went into overtime!